STACEY'S EMERGENCY

**Other books by
Ann M. Martin**

Rachel Parker, Kindergarten Show-off
Eleven Kids, One Summer
Ma and Pa Dracula
Yours Turly, Shirley
Ten Kids, No Pets
Slam Book
Just a Summer Romance
Missing Since Monday
With You and Without You
Me and Katie (the Pest)
Stage Fright
Inside Out
Bummer Summer

BABY-SITTERS LITTLE SISTER series
THE BABY-SITTERS CLUB mysteries
THE BABY-SITTERS CLUB series

STACEY'S EMERGENCY

Ann M. Martin

AN
APPLE
PAPERBACK

SCHOLASTIC INC.
New York Toronto London Auckland Sydney

The author would like to thank
Dr. Claudia Werner
for her sensitive evaluation of this book.

Cover art by Hodges Soileau

ISBN 0-590-74243-4

12 11 10 9 8 7 6 5   7   9/9 0 1/0

Printed in the U.S.A.   40

CHAPTER 1

I looked up from my homework. I watched Charlotte Johanssen, my baby-sitting charge. Charlotte is eight years old.

She was reading *The New York Times*.

She had just finished going through the *Stoneybrook News*.

"Wow," said Charlotte.

"What?" I asked her.

"It says here that in New York this woman had a gun and she — "

"Stop!" I cried. "I don't want to hear about it! And why are you reading that story, anyway?"

"I don't know. It's right here in the paper."

I guess I couldn't fault Charlotte for reading something great (and grown-up) like the *Times*. But did she have to read the grisly stuff? And did she have to read it aloud?

"Gosh," said Charlotte. "*Here* it says that

1

there was a huge fire in a big, fancy hotel one night and — "

"Char! I really don't want to hear about it. . . . Okay?"

"Okay. Actually, I was looking for science articles. Oh, here's one! Hey, Stacey! There's a whole article about diabetes."

"Really?" Now I was interested. That's because I have diabetes myself. Diabetes is a disease. If your blood sugar level gets too high, you can become really sick. There are different kinds of diabetes and different ways to treat the disease. Some people just stick to a low-sugar diet. Other people have to have injections every day. (I'm one of those people. I know giving yourself shots sounds gross, but the shots save my life.) The injections are of insulin, which is what the pancreas (that's a gland in your body) produces to break down sugar. When your body's natural insulin isn't working right, then sometimes you have to give *yourself* insulin. From outside your body. But that doesn't always work. Natural insulin is more effective.

I am lucky in one way because I *can* give myself insulin. Before doctors knew how to do that, I guess people with diabetes suffered a lot. But I am unlucky in another way: I have a severe form of diabetes. My mom told me recently that I'm called a brittle diabetic. That

2

means that my disease is hard to control. I have to have the insulin shots *and* stay on a strict diet. And I mean strict. My mom helps me count calories. This is complicated. We don't simply count calories. We count different *kinds* of calories, like proteins and fats, and we have to balance them. Plus, I have to test my blood. And I have to do it several times each day. How do I test my blood? I prick my finger (I know — you're thinking that diabetes is all shots and finger sticks), then I squeeze out a drop of blood, wipe it on this thing called a test strip, and put the test strip into a machine. A number comes up on the machine, and the number tells me if the level of sugar in my blood is too high (either because I've misjudged and eaten something that has a lot of natural sugar in it, like fruit, or because I have too little insulin in my body), too low (not *enough* sugar in my blood; everybody needs some), or just right.

A few times recently I've seen some numbers that haven't been what they should be. Plus, lately, I've been hungrier and thirstier than usual — and also tired. (I've had some sore throats and stuff, too.) I haven't told Mom about the blood tests, though. She's been through a lot in the past months. (My parents just got divorced, but I'll explain about that later.) I don't want Mom to have to worry about me as well as everything else. Anyway, I'm thirteen years old, and I know my body is going through lots of chemical changes. (Everyone's does when they reach puberty.) So maybe the insulin was just another chemical in my body that was changing — reacting differently to my diet and injections. That is what I *wanted* to believe, but it was my own theory. To tell you the truth, I didn't want to worry Mom because *I* was already worried.

"What does the article say, Char?" I asked her.

"Oh, it's sort of boring." Charlotte skimmed down the page. "It's nothing about treating diabetes. It's about how scientists need more money for research so they can study the disease." Charlotte folded up the paper. Then she reopened it and began looking at the headlines again.

Charlotte Johanssen is really smart. She's an only child, and her parents spend as much time with her as possible — but that isn't a lot. They both work hard, especially Charlotte's mother, who's a doctor. Charlotte's teachers once asked the Johanssens if they'd let Char skip a grade — which Dr. and Mr. Johanssen finally said yes to. It was a big decision. Charlotte may be smart, but she's shy and clingy (although not as bad as she used to be) and has a little trouble making friends.

Sometimes she can be awfully serious, too, which is why I said then, "Hey, Char, let's read something more fun than the paper."

"Okay," she agreed. "Can I see what's in your Kid-Kit?"

A Kid-Kit is a box full of my old toys, books, and games, plus some new things, such as art materials. I bring the Kid-Kit with me on sitting jobs. I wish I could take credit for this great idea, but it wasn't mine. Kristy Thomas, the president and founder of the Baby-sitters Club (which I belong to), thought up Kid-Kits — and a lot of other things as well. But I'll tell you about Kristy and the BSC later, along with my parents' divorce.

Charlotte poked through the Kid-Kit. She pulled out the first book she saw. "Oh, Paddington," she said, sounding disappointed. "We've already read this one."

"Keep looking," I told her.

Char did. Finally she emerged with *The Dancing Cats of Applesap*. "This is a new book, Stacey! Cool!"

"Do you want me to read to you?" (Of course, Charlotte could read the book perfectly well by herself, but there's nothing like being read *to*, no matter how old you are.)

"Yes!" said Charlotte, jumping to her feet.

We both moved to the couch, and Char snuggled next to me while I began reading. I glanced at her a couple of times, because she was *so* engrossed.

Charlotte and I could practically be sisters. Not because we look alike (we don't), but because that's how close we are. Charlotte even stayed at my house once when her parents suddenly had to go out of town for a few days. Maybe I shouldn't say this, but Char is my favorite sitting charge — and I'm her favorite sitter. We mean more to each other than that, though, which is why I think of us as sisters.

Also, I wish I really did have a sister or a brother. But like Charlotte, I'm an only child. And since my parents' divorce, I live mostly with my mother.

Maybe this would be a good time to tell you about the divorce. But beware, it's complicated! Oh, well. Here goes. I grew up in New York City. My dad has a big-time job there. But just before I was going to enter seventh grade, the company he works for transferred him to Stamford, Connecticut, so my parents went house hunting and found a place for us here in Stoneybrook, which is not far from Stamford. Then, in the middle of this school year (eighth grade), the company transferred Dad *back* to New York. (I didn't mind much. I had joined the BSC and made friends in Connecticut, but I also wanted to return to New York and live in the city that felt like home to me.) However, we hadn't been back in New York for more than a few months when my parents began to have problems with each other. They were always fighting. And the next thing I knew, they were getting a divorce. Worse, my father was staying in New York, my mother wanted to return to Connecticut (she *loves* Stoneybrook), and I was given the choice of where I wanted to live. (In other words, with which parent I wanted to live.) It was an awful decision, but finally I chose Connecticut, promising my dad I would visit him on weekends and vacations — whenever I could. I've been *pretty* good about that, but lately, what with feeling tired and cranky and just not *well*, I haven't gone to New York as often as Dad would like. All my energy goes into baby-sitting, school, and homework. I can't think about traveling. It wears me out.

Plus, I feel as though Mom and Dad have been using me a little. I know that's a terrible thing to say about your own parents, but it's true. And it makes me resent the divorce even more, which makes me want to stay put in Connecticut. I'm not trying to punish my dad, I'm just trying to feel like a normal kid with one home. Each time I have to get on the train and *travel* to see my father, I'm reminded of the divorce. I don't like to think of myself as a divorced kid, even though the parents of half of my friends are divorced, too.

Oh. I got off the track. I started to say that I feel like Mom and Dad are using me. By that I mean that they're putting me in the middle. In the middle of them. For instance, when I come home from New York, Mom usually wants to know what Dad's "up to." After a few more questions, I can tell that what she really wants to know is whether Dad is dating someone. Dad does the same thing to me on my weekend visits. What am I supposed to do? In the first place, I usually don't know the answers to their questions. In the second place, when I do know, if I tell, am I being an informant? Is one parent going to call the other and say, "Stacey told me you went out with so-and-so the other night"? And then will I be in trouble?

"Stacey?" asked Charlotte. "Are you okay? You stopped reading."

"Oh, Char, I'm sorry," I told her. "My mind was wandering. Let's see. Where was I?" I'd been reading without paying any attention.

"Right here," said Charlotte, pointing to a spot on page nine.

"Okay." I began reading again. This time I kept my mind on the book. In fact, Charlotte and I both became so caught up in the story that when Dr. Johanssen returned, she startled us!

After I'd been paid (and also after I'd lent Charlotte *The Dancing Cats of Applesap* because she couldn't bear not knowing the end of the story), I asked Dr. Johanssen if I could talk to her in private.

"Of course," said Charlotte's mother, and we sat down in the kitchen.

"It's my diabetes," I blurted out. "I'm tired all the time, hungrier and thirstier than I should be, and . . . and . . ." I finally managed to admit to her that I'd been getting funny blood sugar readings.

I was afraid Dr. Johanssen might blow up at me for ignoring all this stuff. She's not my doctor, but she's *a* doctor, and she's told me I can always go to her when I have questions. But Dr. Johanssen didn't blow up. (I should have known she wouldn't. She's not an explosive person.)

However, she did say, "I think you should have this checked out *soon*, Stacey. You're awfully busy, you're under a lot of stress, and you do have a tricky form of diabetes. Why don't you ask your mom to call your doctor in New York? Or make an appointment to see your doctor, since you're going to visit your dad in a few days."

"Okay," I replied. "Thanks, Doctor Johanssen."

"Any time, honey."

I called good-bye to Charlotte then and left the Johanssens' house. I had intended to go home and catch up on some of my homework. Besides, I was *ravenous*. I could have eaten a horse. Maybe two. Even so, I suddenly didn't feel like going home. I wanted to be with someone — in particular with my best friend, Claudia Kishi. I needed to talk to her.

I needed an escape.

CHAPTER 2

Claudia and I have been best friends since that day at the beginning of seventh grade when we ran into each other. (I mean, actually *ran into* each other.) We realized we were dressed alike — in *very* trendy clothes — and somehow we hit it off. Then when Kristy Thomas, one of Claud's friends, wanted to start a baby-sitting club, I was asked to join. So I became friends with Kristy and *her* best friend, Mary Anne Spier, as well. But Claudia is *my* best friend. (Well, she's my best Connecticut friend. My best New York friend is Laine Cummings. I usually see her when I visit my father.) Anyway, like most best friends, Claudia and I are similar in some ways and different in some ways. We're similar in that (I hope this doesn't sound stuck-up; I just think it's true) we are both pretty sophisticated for thirteen. We wear really fresh clothes — leggings, cowboy boots, oversized shirts, hats

(Claud wears hats more than I do), and wild jewelry. Claudia, who is an excellent artist, makes some of our jewelry herself. Both Claud and I are pretty interested in boys (I've been described as "boy-crazy"), and we like *action!* But that's where the similarities end.

We look different as different can be. I have blue eyes and blonde hair, and my mother allows me to get perms, so my hair is usually fluffy or curly. Claudia, on the other hand, is Japanese-American. She's got these beautiful, very dark, almond-shaped eyes; creamy, un-blemished skin; and long, black, silky hair. While I wear my hair pretty much the same way each day, Claud is forever experimenting with hers. She braids it, puts it in clips, swoops it over to one side of her head in a big ponytail, etc. And she loves weaving rib-bons into her hair, buying or making fancy barrettes, and trying out scarves, headbands, you name it. Then, while I'm an only child in a family that seems pretty mixed up right now, Claud comes from a regular old family. She grew up here in Stoneybrook, and she lives with her parents and her older sister, Janine. Janine is a genius. I mean, a real one with an I.Q. that's way over 150, which is the genius mark. She goes to Stoneybrook High School, but she takes classes at our local college. Can you imagine? Sixteen and taking college courses? I don't know why she doesn't just go off to college right now and forget the rest of high school. If she did, she would certainly make life easier for Claudia. That's because, although Claud is smart, she's a terrible student — and an even worse speller. I think that school just doesn't interest her. What does interest her is art. Claud is very talented. As I mentioned earlier, she makes jewelry. She also paints, draws, sculpts, and sometimes experiments with pottery. Her work has even won some local awards. Another thing Claud likes is reading Nancy Drew mysteries. Her parents, however, think she should be reading classics or something. (Mrs. Kishi is a librarian.) But Claud just loves mysteries, so she buys the books anyway and hides them around her room. Along with junk food, which she's addicted to. Her room can be pretty interesting. You reach into a container labeled PAPER CLIPS and pull out a handful of root beer barrels. You open a desk drawer, looking for a pencil, and find a bag of M&M's. You ask Claud about the latest book she's read — and she retrieves it from the folds of a quilt at the end of her bed. Claudia is fun, funny, generous, and talented. I just wish she had higher self-esteem.

Talk about self-esteem, Kristy Thomas has it, despite what *she's* been through in the last year or so. You think my family is mixed up? Wait until you hear about Kristy's. Kristy, the president of the Baby-sitters Club, used to live across the street from Claud. She lived there with her mother and her three brothers — Charlie and Sam, who are in high school, and David Michael, who is seven. Mr. Thomas had walked out on the family when Kristy was six or seven (I think). He just walked out, leaving Kristy's mom to raise four kids. Which she did. She got herself together and found a good job with a company in Stamford. Then, a few months before Kristy entered seventh grade, her mother began dating this millionaire, Watson Brewer. He was the first guy Mrs. Thomas had been serious about since her husband left. And he was the first guy that Kristy said she didn't like. Watson had been married once before, and he had two children, Andrew and Karen, who are four and seven now. During the summer between seventh and eighth grade, Mrs. Thomas married Watson. (That's how I always think of him, because that's what Kristy calls him.) After the wedding, Watson moved Kristy and her family from their small house into his mansion across town. Naturally, Kristy resented this, even though everyone in the family has a room to himself or herself, including Karen and Andrew, who live with their father only every other week-end.

Guess what. Not long ago, Watson and Mrs. Thomas adopted a little girl. They named her Emily Michelle. She's two and a half, and she comes from Vietnam. She's adorable. With such a little kid around, though, arrangements had to be made for someone to be at home while the adults were at work and everyone else was at school. So Nannie, Kristy's grandmother, joined the household. What with Kristy, her mom, her brothers, her stepfather, her stepsister and stepbrother, her adopted sister, her grandmother, and the pets (a cat, a dog, and two goldfish), the Brewer/Thomas house is wild, crazy . . . and wonderful! (Even Kristy admits that now.)

Kristy herself is outgoing (she's noted for her big mouth), a tomboy, and just a little immature compared to the rest of us in the BSC. She doesn't care a thing about clothes and almost always wears jeans, a turtleneck shirt, a sweater or sweat shirt, and running shoes. Sometimes she wears her baseball cap with the collie on it. She's pretty, although I don't think she knows it. Best of all, when you dig below the loudmouth exterior, you find a caring, concerned, organized person, full of good ideas and creativity. (Needless to say,

Kristy — like the rest of us — *loves* kids.)

Kristy's best friend, Mary Anne Spier, actually looks a little like Kristy. They're both short for their age (Kristy is shorter) and have brown hair and brown eyes. Their features are even similar. But beyond looks, they are two extremely different people. While Kristy is outgoing, Mary Anne is shy. She has trouble speaking up for herself or voicing her opinions, although she's better about that than she was when I first met her. She's a romantic and cries easily. (Never see a sad movie with her.) She even had a steady boyfriend for a long time.

Mary Anne grew up next door to Kristy. (She's moved, too, though. I'll explain in a minute.) But her home life was certainly different from Kristy's. It was quiet (no brothers leaping around), just Mary Anne and her dad. Mary Anne's mom died when Mary Anne was quite little. She barely remembers her mother. Mary Anne was raised by Mr. Spier, who was awfully strict with her. Not that he's mean, but he does have this thing about orderliness and neatness and organization. Also, I think he wanted to prove to everyone that he could raise a little girl all by himself just fine. So he invented these rules for Mary Anne and practically took over her life. When I first met Mary Anne she seemed like such a little girl, even though she's my age. That changed when Mary Anne was able to show her father that she was as mature as the rest of her friends. Then he loosened up on her, and Mary Anne loosened up, too.

Midway through seventh grade, a new girl, Dawn Schafer, moved to Stoneybrook — all the way from California. Dawn, a member of the BSC now, had moved here with her mother and younger brother, Jeff, after her parents had gotten divorced. (Sound familiar?) Her mom had chosen Stoneybrook because she grew up here and Dawn's grandparents still live here. Our California girl has the most amazingly blonde hair I've ever seen. And it's *long*. Her eyes are a sparkly blue, and, well, she's striking-looking. Dawn hates the cold Connecticut winters, loves the warm summers and health food, and is into exercising. Also, she has always liked ghost stories. This is interesting, considering that Dawn's mother bought an *old* (colonial) farmhouse, which has a secret passage that just may be haunted. (We're not sure.) Dawn is self-assured and an individualist. She doesn't care much what other people think about her. And she dresses in her own casual-trendy, one-of-a-kind style.

Anyway, shortly after Dawn moved here, she and Mary Anne became friends. Now they're stepsisters. How did that happen?

Well, Dawn and Mary Anne are partially responsible. They were looking through some old Stoneybrook High yearbooks and discovered that Mary Anne's father and Dawn's mother had been high-school sweethearts. But after graduation, they went in different directions. So Dawn and Mary Anne found a way for their parents to meet again, Mrs. Schafer and Mr. Spier began dating, and after what seemed like forever, they got married! Then Mary Anne, her father, and her kitten, Tigger, moved into Dawn's house. (Jeff wasn't there, though. He had never adjusted to his new life and had returned to California to live with his dad.) Now Dawn and Mary Anne are living under the same roof, which has been difficult sometimes, but mostly just fine.

While Claudia, Kristy, Mary Anne, Dawn, and I are all thirteen and in eighth grade, the two other BSC members are eleven and in sixth grade. Their names are Jessi (short for Jessica) Ramsey and Mallory (usually known as Mal) Pike. And *they* are best friends, too. (I think it's interesting that there are so many pairs of best friends in the BSC, yet we get along well as a group.) Anyway, Jessi and Mal are both the oldest kids in their families, they *love* to read (especially horse stories, and especially the ones by Marguerite Henry), they also like to write (Mallory more so than Jessi), and they both feel that their parents treat them like infants, even though they are old enough to baby-sit, and old enough for plenty of other things. I remember being eleven. It wasn't a great age.

Jessi comes from a pretty average family. She lives with her parents, her Aunt Cecelia, her eight-year-old sister, Becca (Charlotte Johanssen's best friend), and her baby brother, Squirt. Guess where her family lives. In *my* old house! The one I lived in before we went back to New York and my parents got divorced. (Jessi's family moved here from New Jersey.) Jessi is a really talented ballet dancer. I've seen her perform. She's used to dancing onstage in front of big audiences, and she takes lessons at a school in Stamford that she had to audition for just to be allowed to enroll. Jessi has long dark eyelashes, big brown eyes, legs that go on forever, and chocolatey brown skin.

Mal, on the other hand, comes from a huge family. She has *seven* younger brothers and sisters, three of whom are identical triplets (boys). Mal's passion is writing. Also drawing. She'd like to write and illustrate children's books one day. Mal is not feeling too pretty at the moment. She's got wavy red hair (her hair and face *are* pretty), but she's also got glasses and braces. Her braces, at least, are the clear plastic kind, so they don't show up too much. Mal's parents will *not* let her wear contacts instead of glasses. They did, however, finally let her get her ears pierced (the Ramseys let Jessi do the same), so there's hope. Besides, the braces will come off eventually.

So there you are. Those are my friends: Kristy, Dawn, Mallory, Jessi, Mary Anne, and Claudia, my best friend, with whom I needed to talk pretty desperately. She lives not far from Charlotte, and I was hoping she'd be at home.

CHAPTER 3

Claudia was at home and we had a nice talk. There's something comforting about Claud's room, as well as about Claudia herself. Maybe that's one reason the Baby-sitters Club meets there.

I guess now I ought to tell you just what the BSC is, since I've mentioned it several times. The club was Kristy's idea. She got it back at the beginning of seventh grade, when her mom was first dating Watson, and just after I'd moved to Stoneybrook (for the first time). In those days (they seem so long ago, but they really weren't), Kristy and Mary Anne still lived next door to each other and across the street from Claud. And Kristy and her older brothers were responsible for taking turns watching David Michael after school. That was a good arrangement — as long as one of them was free each afternoon. Of course, they weren't always free. And one evening, when Kristy, Sam, and Charlie had realized that they were all busy the next day, Kristy sat eating pizza and watching her mom make one phone call after another, trying to line up a baby-sitter for David Michael. Unfortunately, David Michael was watching, too, and Kristy felt sorry for him. (David Michael knew he was the source of some sort of trouble.) Too bad, thought Kristy, that her mom couldn't make just one phone call and reach a whole lot of sitters at once. And that was when she got one of the great ideas she's famous for. She and her friends could start a baby-sitting business! If they met somewhere a few times a week, parents could call them and, just as Kristy had imagined, reach several sitters at the same time. Somebody was bound to be free (and get a job), and the parent would be satisfied. So Kristy called Claud and Mary Anne, and they decided to start the Baby-sitters Club.

Right away, the girls realized that a fourth member would be a good idea. Claud suggested me, since she and I were already getting to know each other and I'd done a lot of sitting in New York. And so the BSC was ready and running. Well, almost. We had to do a lot of work in the beginning. First, we planned to meet three afternoons each week in Claud's room (she has her own phone); on

Monday, Wednesday, and Friday, from five-thirty until six. Parents could call us on Claud's line during those times and reach four experienced baby-sitters. But how would they know about our meetings?

"We'll advertise," said Kristy.

So we advertised. We told practically everyone about the BSC. We sent out fliers. We even placed an ad in the *Stoneybrook News*. And when we held our first official meeting, we actually got job calls. After that, the calls kept coming, and they haven't stopped. In fact, we started getting so many that the club had to expand. Dawn joined us after she moved to Connecticut. Then, when I had to go back to New York, Kristy asked both Jessi and Mal to join. And then I returned. I was allowed back into the club. I became the seventh member, and I think I'll be the last. (Unless someone else has to leave.) Claudia's bedroom can't hold more than seven people. Well, comfortably. We'd have to figure out how to drape new people around the ceiling.

The BSC is run very efficiently. Kristy makes sure of that. She's our president. The rest of us are officers, too, and we each have our own job or function. Kristy is president because the club was her idea. That makes sense. Also, Kristy is the kind of person who's good at running things. And with the great ideas she's always getting, she keeps coming up with new ways to promote the club, to attract more clients, or to run the club even *more* efficiently. (Sometimes she goes overboard, but the rest of us let her know right away.)

Claudia is the vice-president. She should be, since the members of the club swarm into her bedroom three times a week, eat her junk food, and tie up her phone. Also, parents sometimes call Claud's line during nonmeeting times, and Claudia has to deal with those job appointments on her own.

The secretary of the club is Mary Anne. She's neat and organized — thank goodness. Sometimes I think she works harder than anyone else at a meeting. Her job is to keep the record book up-to-date and in order. The record book was one of Kristy's ideas. In it, Mary Anne keeps track of our clients — their names, addresses, phone numbers, rates paid, and special information about their children. More important, she schedules every baby-sitting job that comes in. That means that she has to know all of our schedules — when Jessi has ballet lessons or Claud has an art class or Mal has an orthodontist appointment. I don't think Mary Anne has ever made a scheduling boo-boo.

I am the club treasurer. Not to brag, but I happen to be very good at math. It just comes easily to me. I can add up numbers in a flash — in my head. My job is to collect the club dues from every member each Monday, to put the money in our treasury (a manila envelope), and then to dole out the money as it's needed. What do we use the money for? Lots of things. To help Claud pay her monthly phone bill, to pay Charlie Thomas to drive Kristy back and forth to meetings now that she lives too far away to get to Claud's on her own, to fund an occasional club party, and to restock the Kid-Kits when we run out of things such as crayons or stickers. Remember my Kid-Kit? Well, we each have one. They're great baby-sitting tools. We don't bring them along *every* time we sit, but pretty often. The kids love them, so their parents see happy faces when they come home — and then they're more apt to turn to the BSC the next time they need a sitter.

Dawn's position is alternate officer of the BSC. That means that she can take over the job of anyone who misses a meeting. And *that* means that Dawn has to be familiar with the duties of each officer. I know that sounds difficult, but it isn't really that bad. Anyway, the BSC members don't miss meetings very often. So Dawn answers the telephone a lot.

Jessi and Mallory are junior officers. This is because they are eleven and not allowed to sit

25

at night unless they're taking care of their own brothers and sisters. They are a huge help, though. By taking over a lot of the afternoon jobs, they free up us older members for the nighttime jobs.

Hmm. Let me see. A couple of other things about the workings of the BSC . . .

Just in case a call should come in that *none* of us can take (and that does happen every now and then), Kristy signed on two associate members of the club. These are reliable sitters who don't go to meetings, but whom we can call on in a pinch so that we won't have to disappoint our clients. Our associate members are Shannon Kilbourne, a friend of Kristy's in her new neighborhood, and Logan Bruno. He's the guy Mary Anne used to go steady with!

Finally, an*other* of Kristy's ideas was to keep a club notebook. The notebook is more like a diary. In it, each member is responsible for writing up every job she goes on. Then we're supposed to read the notebook once a week to catch up on what's happening with our clients, and also to see how our friends have handled sticky sitting situations. No one likes writing in the notebook much (except Mallory), but we have to agree that it's pretty helpful.

* * *

26

"Ahem!"

It was later in the afternoon. Claud and I had finished our talk, and now all of my friends and I had gathered together. Kristy was sitting straight and tall (well, as tall as she could make herself) in Claudia's director's chair. She was wearing her presidential visor and, as usual, a pencil was stuck over one ear.

"Ahem!" Kristy cleared her throat again loudly. She did not have a cold. She was signaling to the rest of us that it was 5:31 according to Claud's digital alarm clock, the official BSC timepiece, and reminding us that she'd called the day's meeting to order a full minute earlier.

What were the rest of us doing? Jessi and Mal were sitting on the floor, leaning against the bed and playing with these paper fortune-telling things they'd made (that, for some reason, they called Cootie Catchers). They kept opening and closing them and reciting, "Eenie, meenie, minie, moe. Catch a tiger by the toe. If he roars then let him go. Eenie, meenie, minie, moe. My mother said to pick just one, and this . . . is . . . it!" Then they'd read a fortune written under a flap of paper. (Cootie Catchers are hard to explain.) Claudia, Mary Anne, and I were lined up on Claud's bed, leaning against the wall. And Dawn was straddling Claud's desk chair, sitting in it backward, her chin resting on the top rung.

Claud had unearthed some packages of Ring-Dings and was passing them around. The smell of chocolate was driving me crazy. At least I wasn't the only one not eating them, though. Dawn wouldn't touch them. She nibbled at some crackers instead. I did, too, but the crackers didn't begin to quiet the rumbling in my *very* hungry stomach — too hungry for that time of day. A Ring-Ding or two might have taken care of things.

Anyway when Kristy began her throat-clearing, we sat at attention. And just in time. The phone rang. Dawn answered it.

"Hello, Baby-sitters Club . . . Hi, Dr. Johanssen . . . Next Tuesday? I'll have Mary Anne check. I'll get right back to you. . . . Okay. 'Bye." Dawn hung up and faced the rest of us. "Sitter for Charlotte next Tuesday night from seven till ten."

While Mary Anne looked at the appointment pages in the record book, Jessi and Mal let out groans. A nighttime sitting job. Neither of them could take it. They were disappointed.

"Okay," said Mary Anne, glancing up. "Stacey, Kristy, and Dawn are free."

"I've got a history test the next day," said Dawn. "I better stay at home where I can really concentrate while I'm studying."

"You take the job then, Stace," said Kristy.

"You live much closer to Char."

So I got the job. Mary Anne penciled it into the record book, and Dawn phoned Dr. Johanssen to tell her who the sitter would be. That's how we always schedule jobs. Diplomatically. (Okay, *usually*. But we hardly ever have fights at meetings.)

The rest of the half hour passed busily. The phone rang a lot. (Twice, though, the calls were from Sam Thomas, goofing on us.) At six o'clock, Kristy jumped to her feet, announcing, "Meeting adjourned!"

We all stood up. Mal and Jessi took out their Cootie Catchers again. Kristy looked out the window to see if Charlie had arrived to pick her up. Dawn and Mary Anne hurried toward the door, and Claudia followed them. It was her turn to help with dinner that night.

Since no one was watching, I stuck my hand in the dresser drawer where I'd seen Claudia rehide the Ring-Dings.

I pulled out a package and snuck it into my purse.

CHAPTER 4

Ring, ring.

I could hear the telephone in my mother's room. Why doesn't s̲h̲e̲ answer it? I wondered, feeling cranky. Then I remembered that Mom had run over to the Pikes'. (Mallory's house is behind ours. Her back windows face our back windows.) Mom had said she'd be home in fifteen or twenty minutes.

So I would have to get the phone.

"Yuck," I said as I sat up. It was a Wednesday evening. I was lying on my bed, trying to find the energy to start my homework. I hadn't found it yet.

Ring, ring!

The telephone actually sounded impatient. I struggled to my feet and hurried into Mom's room.

"Hello?" I said, placing the receiver to my ear.

"Hi, Boontsie." It was Dad, using his awful baby name for me.

"Hi, Dad!" I tried to sound perky rather than dead tired.

"How are you doing? Are you ready for the weekend?"

"Sure," I replied. The upcoming weekend was a Dad Weekend. (I had conveniently forgotten to call my doctor.) I would leave for New York on Friday afternoon, missing a BSC meeting. (Dawn would get to be the treasurer that day.)

"What train are you taking?" asked Dad.

"The one that gets in at six-oh-four," I replied.

"Great. I'll meet you at the Information Booth at Grand Central then."

"Oh, Dad. You don't have to meet me," I said. (We have this discussion practically every time I go to New York.) "I can get a cab to your apartment."

"You won't have time. I made six-thirty dinner reservations."

"But I'll have all my stuff with me," I pointed out, trying not to whine. "I don't want to lug it around some restaurant."

"Don't worry. You can check your things with our coats. Then we'll have a nice leisurely dinner before we go home."

"Okay." Inwardly I sighed. I had a feeling

that Dad had made lots of plans for the weekend. Sometimes that's okay. But not when I'm so tired. And not when I have a mountain of homework to catch up on. I'd been planning to do some of it in New York. Oh, well. I could work on the train. (I'd be spending three and a half or four hours on the train that weekend.)

Dad *did* have a lot of plans. It turned out that he'd bought tickets to a Broadway musical for Saturday night. He knew about special exhibits at practically every museum in New York. And he'd made reservations for about sixteen hundred meals. (I don't think my father ever cooks for himself. His refrigerator looks like a hole: empty.)

"Will I get to see Laine sometime?" I asked.

"Sure. She can come to the MOMA with us." (The MOMA is the Museum of Modern Art. It is not Laine's favorite place.)

"Dad? Maybe we could skip the MOMA on Saturday afternoon? Then Laine could come over and we could just hang out and talk."

"Is that really how you want to spend Saturday?" asked Dad.

"Just the afternoon." I yawned.

"You sound awfully tired, honey."

"I guess I am, a little. I've got a lot of schoolwork." I almost said to Dad then, "Couldn't we cancel this weekend so I could stay at home and rest and catch up on things?" But I knew I'd hurt his feelings if I did that.

"Well, try to get some extra sleep," said Dad matter-of-factly. "We've got a big weekend ahead of us."

Tell me about it, I thought. "Okay," I said.

"So I'll meet you at Grand Central at a little after six."

"Right." I stifled another yawn.

There was a pause. Then Dad said, "Is your mother there?"

"No." I didn't mean to sound evasive. I was thinking about the weekend that lay ahead, mentally trying to conjure up some energy.

"Where is she?" asked Dad suspiciously.

Uh-oh. He was going to do it again.

"She's at the Pikes'."

"At this hour?"

"Dad, it's eight-thirty."

"Well, what's she doing over there? And why are you at home alone?"

Oh, brother. I tried to sidestep what was coming by saying, "I've been able to stay at home alone for several years now. Sometimes I even baby-sit."

"Anastasia," said Dad. (Yikes, my full name.) "You know what I mean. Why is your mother at the Pikes' on a weeknight without you?"

"Because she and Mrs. Pike are friends."

Why did I always end up defending my parents to each other? And what if Mom *were* out on a date? She's allowed to date. She and my father are divorced, for heaven's sake.

"What does that mean?" asked Dad.

"It means that Mrs. Pike got a new dress and she wants Mom's opinion."

"Why?"

"Because she wants to get a hat to go with it or something. *I* don't know." I felt extremely exasperated.

"You're sure she's at the Pikes'?"

"*Da-ad.*"

"Okay. Just wondering."

And *I* was wondering what would happen if one day I said to my father, "Mom's out with someone. A *man*. He's taking her to dinner. He's *really* handsome, he has a very important job, and he's never been married. He's saving himself for the perfect woman, and that perfect woman is Mom." Or what would happen if I said to my mother some Sunday night when she was grilling me about my weekend in New York with Dad, "Mom, you should *see* who Dad's dating. She's this sophisticated, beautiful, *younger* woman. She's terribly wealthy, she has a penthouse apartment in the city and a horse farm in the country. And she can cook *and* handle a jigsaw."

If I ever said anything like that, would my

parents be mad at *me?* I didn't want to find out.

"Stacey?" Dad was saying.

"Yeah?"

"You didn't answer me. I asked how school was going."

"Oh, it's fine."

"And the Baby-sitters Club?"

"Fine." I heard a door downstairs open and close. "Hey, Mom's home!" I exclaimed. Now I could show Dad that I'd been telling the truth.

"Can you put her on for a minute?" he asked.

"Sure. Oh, and I'll see you on Friday. 'Bye, Dad. Hold on for Mom." I went to the head of the staircase and yelled, "Hey, Mom! Dad's on the phone. He wants to talk to you!" Then I dashed back to her bedroom. I didn't give my mother a chance to whisper frantically to me that she didn't want to talk to my father. If I had to get back on the phone and make an excuse for her, Dad would be *sure* something was going on.

In Mom's bedroom, I did the first of two things that I really should not have done that night. I listened to my parents' conversation.

When Mom picked up the phone in the kitchen, Dad greeted her with, "Did you decide on a hat?" He thought he was being

35

cagey. If Mom didn't know what he was talking about, then Dad could assume she'd been out somewhere with Wonder Date.

"A hat?" Mom repeated. "For Mrs. Pike? Yes. Why?"

"Oh, never mind." Dad didn't really have anything to say after that, so he and Mom just went over the plans for my weekend in the city. I waited until they'd said good-bye. After each of them had hung up the phone, I hung up the extension I'd been listening in on. Then I crept back to my room.

I lay down on my bed. My stomach was growling, and I desperately wanted something to drink — even though Mom and I had finished our dinner not too much earlier. I didn't want to go to the kitchen, though. I had a feeling Mom would be mad at me for having called her to the phone. Plus, did she know, somehow, that I'd eavesdropped?

I had to give her time to cool off.

I also had to eat something . . . anything. So I tiptoed across the room, gently closed the door, and then tiptoed to my desk. Feeling like Claudia, I pulled out a drawer, lifted up a pile of papers, opened an old pencil box, and removed — a large chocolate bar.

Ah, sugar, I thought.

I peeled back the top of the paper and, for

a second, just breathed in the incredible smell of chocolate.

I was tired. *Sick* and tired, I reminded myself. And I was sick and tired of being sick and tired. Nobody else I knew had to stick to a diet like mine. Dawn didn't touch junk food, but that was *her* decision. My diet was *not my* decision.

Oh, I had longed for the taste of chocolate again. I had not had *any* since the doctors first discovered that I was diabetic. Claudia's Ring-Dings had tasted out of this world. When I'd eaten them, I'd felt as if I were tasting chocolate for the first time.

So I ate the entire candy bar.

Then I felt guilty.

I just couldn't win.

CHAPTER 5

The next day, after school, I sat for Charlotte again. Charlotte wasn't her usual quiet self. She wanted to *do* something, to *create* something.

"Like what?" I asked, thinking of arts and crafts and wishing I'd brought along my Kid-Kit that afternoon. "A painting?"

"No. Something more complicated."

Char and I were sitting opposite each other at the Johanssens' kitchen table. Charlotte grew thoughtful.

"More complicated? How about a paper sculpture?" I suggested.

Charlotte considered. Finally, she shook her head slowly and said, "I think I want to make fudge."

Fudge? Really? Of all things, why did Charlotte want to make fudge? I didn't think I could stand being within a mile of something chocolate and not eating it. Fudge making would be torture.

"Not paper sculpture?" I asked lamely.

"No, fudge. Please, Stacey? Puh-*lease?* We've got all the ingredients. And Becca could come over and help me. We would have so much fun. We could pretend we were chefs in a famous restaurant and that people came from miles around for our special dessert — fudge."

How could I ignore that? "Okay. Call Becca," I said, hiding my disappointment.

"Thank you, thank you, thank you!" Charlotte cried. She was on the phone in an instant. "Hi, Becca, it's me," she said. (I smiled, thinking that only really good friends can do that.) "Stacey's here. She's baby-sitting me. She said I could make fudge. Do you want to come over and help? . . . Okay, I'll see you in a few minutes."

By the time Becca arrived, Charlotte was already assembling ingredients on the kitchen table. Sugar, chocolate . . . *Ohhh.*

"Hi!" said Charlotte excitedly, as Becca entered the kitchen. "I'm Chef Charlotte and you're Chef Becca. We work in the Grand Sparkle-Glitter Hotel. We are famous chefs."

"World famous?" asked Becca, tying on the apron I handed her.

"Galaxy famous," replied Charlotte.

39

"Known on planets everywhere."

"Boy . . ." said Becca.

"Fudge is our specialty," Charlotte went on. "Isn't it, Stacey?"

I smiled. "Yup. And it's a *special* specialty on Saturn."

"No, make it Mars!" cried Becca.

"Okay, on Mars. But why?" I asked.

"Because we could pretend to travel there and be Martian fudge makers. Or we could make Milky Ways."

Charlotte giggled. Then she said, "Wait! I know! Don't start the fudge yet, anybody. I'll be right back!"

Char darted off. Becca and I looked at each other. What could Charlotte possibly be doing? our eyes asked.

We found out in less than a minute. Charlotte scampered back into the kitchen, wearing a pair of waving, bobbing antennae on her head. She handed another set to Becca.

"Put them on!" said Charlotte. "Now we'll really look like Martian fudge makers. Isn't this great?"

"Yeah!" agreed Becca.

So the two Martians set to work. At first I wished I had my camera. I'd never seen anything quite like Becca and Char, wearing antennae on their heads and oversized aprons around their middles, up to their elbows in chocolate goo. But soon my amusement faded.

It was the chocolate smell. I could barely concentrate on anything except that sweet odor. (Torture, torture.) I hoped I didn't look as upset as I felt. And soon I decided I didn't. The girls weren't paying attention to me.

"Look! We're flying by the moon," said Becca.

"Yeah. We should stop there. Did you know that moon dust is a good substitute for sugar? Let's stock up."

"Oh, no! We've gone too far!" cried Becca.

"Stop the rocket ship!" added Charlotte.

This conversation was being held while the girls stood quietly at the table, stirring the fudge in a plastic bowl with wooden spoons. Then:

"Eeeetch!" screeched Becca, imitating the sound of skidding brakes. As she did so, she flung one arm up to her head, as if to protect herself from a crash. Unfortunately, it was the arm that was stirring the fudge, so she flung the spoon up, too. The fudge mixture flew behind her and sprayed the wall over the sink.

"Uh-oh," said Becca. "I didn't mean to do that. Honest."

"I know you didn't. It's okay," I told her. I stood up wearily and headed for the sink. "You guys keep working," I went on. "I'll clean up."

"Thanks," said Becca with a sigh of relief.

While I wet a sponge and began to wipe off the wall, Charlotte and Becca continued their imaginary space game.

"The famous Martian fudge makers!" cried Charlotte.

"Have we reached Mars yet?" asked Becca.

"Not quite. Our spaceship feels . . . Oh, no! We're flying straight toward a huge meteor shower! We're going to crash!"

I turned around. My usually quiet Charlotte was becoming raucous. I almost told her to calm down but decided not to. Char hardly ever let go like this. Maybe it was good for her. So I kept my mouth shut, turned back to the wall, and continued scrubbing.

"A meteor shower!" Becca exclaimed. "What's that?"

"It's a — Wait a sec! We've hit it! . . . *Bam, bam, bam!* Our ship is being bombarded by meteors. One is heading for our windshield. Duck!"

At that moment, I heard the thump. In their excitement, their imaginations completely runaway, the girls had dropped to the floor. And somehow their bowl of fudge had come with them.

Chocolate, chocolate everywhere.

"Oops," said Charlotte.

The girls had stood up and were looking at

me. I had turned around and was looking at them. I sighed.

"Can we start over again?" asked Charlotte in a very small voice.

"If you two clean up this mess," I replied. "And if, when you start the next batch, you promise to be earthling girls, cooking in a nice kitchen in Connecticut. Without antennae."

"We promise," said Charlotte and Becca in unison.

They removed their antennae. I handed them a roll of paper towels and the sponge I'd been using, and they set to work. When the kitchen was clean, they began their project again. Calmly.

At last the fudge was finished.

"Can we taste it?" asked Char. "I know it's too close to dinner to have a whole piece, but can we each have a little sample?"

I smiled. "Sure." I cut each of the girls a tiny square of fudge.

"Yummm," they said, their eyes closed.

Yummmm, I thought. What I wouldn't give for —

"Hey!" cried Becca. "Guess what's on TV *right now?*"

"What?" asked Charlotte.

"That special. The one about the boy and his horse."

"Oh, I want to see that!" exclaimed Char.

Then she added, "But we should help Stacey cut up the fudge."

She sounded completely unenthusiastic. And no wonder. Cutting up something you've just made is the boring part. So I said, "You guys go on and watch the special. I'll cut up the fudge." (I wouldn't have let them cut it up anyway, since you need a sharp knife.)

The girls ran off. I sliced the fudge into small, neat squares.

I set aside a pile for Becca to take home with her.

And then I wrapped two pieces in a napkin and stashed the bundle in my purse.

In my bedroom that night, I tried to concentrate on my homework. How had I gotten so far behind? My teachers were on my back, but at least they hadn't told my mother yet. If I could catch up, she'd probably never have to know.

But I was having trouble keeping my mind on my work. For one thing, I was hungry — again. I thought of the fudge in my purse. Do you know the phrase "money burning a hole in your pocket"? Well, the fudge was burning a hole in my purse. I could not stop thinking about it. At last, I reached into my purse, found the fudge, and ate both pieces. Oh, yum. I *craved* chocolate now. I'd bought a candy bar at school and eaten it secretly in the girls' room that afternoon. And then there was that other candy bar . . . and the Ring-Dings . . .

What was I doing to myself? I wondered. And just then, I realized that I had not yet packed to go to Dad's. I was supposed to leave after school the next day. So I would have to pack now. What a drag. I stood up slowly, went to my closet, and pulled out my overnight bag. I could hear the phone ringing, but Mom was home and she picked it up in her bedroom. When she didn't shout to me that I had a call, I began packing.

I forgot about the telephone completely until I heard Mom's raised voice say, "You are *spoiling* her! I'm not kidding."

Dad must be the one who had called. (I couldn't imagine Mom talking like that to anyone else.) And the "her" who was getting spoiled must be me.

I crept into the hall and tiptoed as close to Mom's room as I dared. I could hear her end of the conversation as clearly as a bell ringing on a quiet night. But her voice didn't sound pleasant and magical the way I thought a nighttime bell might. In a forced whisper (Mom must have realized how loudly she'd been speaking) she said, "Don't *buy* Stacey so many things this weekend. And give her a break. She's been tired recently. She could do with a nice, quiet weekend. . . . What? . . . Well, that's what I'm *saying*. She doesn't need to eat out four or five times *and* go to the theater *and* to museums." There was a long pause. Then Mom said harshly, "I am *not* jealous of what you can do for Stacey. Just give her some time off. . . . All ri-ight," she went on, as if to say, "I know you're going to do everything anyway — and it will be a bad idea." After another, shorter pause, Mom said, "I'll be checking with Stacey on Sunday."

And Dad will be grilling me about Mom, her job, and the nonexistent Wonder Date. That was just great. I couldn't wait to be Stacey-in-the-middle again.

I tiptoed back to my bedroom. There was my half-packed overnight bag. There was my unfinished homework.

I finished packing. Then I put my books away. I stretched out on my bed, even though I was still dressed.

I had a horrible headache.

CHAPTER 6

I was all packed and ready to go. But leaving for New York was the last thing I wanted to do. It wasn't just Mom and Dad and the divorce. It was everything rolled into one: those things, plus school, plus not feeling well. To be honest, I was more concerned about my schoolwork that day than about anything else. I was *so* far behind. I don't know why someone at school — for instance, my guidance counselor, who preferred to think of herself as my "friend" — hadn't called Mom yet. The only grade I was keeping up was math. The others were slipping, and I was in danger of failing French.

Late the night before, when something had been keeping me awake, I'd thought: Oh, no! What if someone at school *has* called my mother, and Mom just hasn't mentioned it because she doesn't want to worry me? What if I'm very sick and everyone knows but me?

. . . That's paranoid, isn't it? I'm just thinking that way because I'm not feeling well and I haven't told Mom, so I have a guilty conscience.

At the end of school on Friday, I'd said to my friends when we gathered in the hall, "I'm sorry I have to miss today's club meeting."

"That's okay," said Kristy. "We understand."

"Boy, I wish *I* were going to New York with you," spoke up Mary Anne wistfully. "Do you think you'll go to the Hard Rock Cafe?"

"With *Dad?*" I replied. "No. We're eating at the Sign of the Dove tonight. And at the Russian Tea Room tomorrow night."

"Sign of the Dove *and* the Russian Tea Room?" squealed Mary Anne. "You're kidding . . . aren't you?"

"Nope."

"What are the Sign of the Dove and the Russian Tea Room?" asked Mallory.

"Only two of the finest dining establishments in New York City," Mary Anne answered. (If she sounded like a guidebook on New York, it's probably because she's read about a million of them. Mary Anne's dream is to live in New York City someday.) She went on, "You are so lucky, Stacey!"

"Dining establishments?" Mallory repeated. "You mean places to eat?"

"Awesome, fresh, *distant* places to eat," replied Mary Anne.

"I doubt if the owners of those restaurants would describe them that way, though," said Dawn.

"No, of course not," agreed Mary Anne, aghast at what she'd said. "They'd use phrases like, 'culinary delights' or . . . 'splendiferous spreads.' "

"Splen*di*ferous *spreads?*" I laughed. I couldn't help it.

"Oh, okay. Then they're just four-star restaurants, at least in *my* book."

"Hey, Stace! There's your mom!" cried Claudia. "Listen, have a *great* weekend. Call me Sunday night when you get back and tell me everything."

"No, wait until Monday!" exclaimed Mary Anne. "Tell all of us about your weekend while we're holding our meeting. We'll want every detail."

"No, *you* will," whispered Kristy, but Mary Anne didn't hear her.

"What you ate, how it was prepared, who you saw in the restaurants. You're bound to spot celebrities," Mary Anne continued excitedly. "If you see anyone *really* famous, try to bring me back a personal souvenir, like a table scrap."

"You mean like a half-eaten piece of bread?"

"Yeah!"

"Mary Anne, that is *so* disgusting," said Jessi.

And Kristy added, "If, for whatever wild reason, I ever wind up as a celebrity, don't let Mary Anne near me."

Mom honked the horn twice then. "I better go," I said. "We're going to be early for the train, but I hate to keep Mom waiting. I'll see you guys on Monday."

We called good-bye to each other, and as my friends walked off, I headed toward Mom and our car. I was carrying a *pile* of books, hoping to get caught up over the weekend.

"Hi!" I said to Mom as I opened the front door. "Did you bring my bag?"

"It's right there in the backseat," Mom answered. "Are you ready for the weekend?" She glanced sideways at me. "You look a little pale."

"Just tired I guess. I didn't sleep much last night. How are you? You didn't have any trouble getting off work early today?"

"Not a bit." Mom smiled.

A half an hour or so later, the train pulled into the Stoneybrook station, where Mom and I had been waiting. She was sipping coffee, and I was finishing up a diet soda.

"Have fun, sweetie!" called Mom, after I'd

kissed her good-bye and was stepping onto the train.

"I will," I answered. I found a seat by a window and waved to Mom as the train ground into motion and my mother and the platform slipped away from me. I looked around. The train wasn't too crowded. In fact, my car was only about half full. Good. Things would be quiet. Maybe I could finally get some work done. I stowed my overnight bag on the floor by my feet, stuck my purse protectively between me and the side of the train, and set my book bag on the empty seat next to me. I reached inside, pulled out my French text, and turned to the chapter in which I'd been goofing up. (That was a number of chapters before the one we were already working on.) "The *pluperfect*," I muttered, and began to read.

The next thing I knew, an announcement was coming over the loudspeaker. "Station stop, Pennington. This is Pennington!"

Pennington! That was more than halfway to New York! I'd fallen asleep and had just wasted over an hour's worth of studying time.

I yawned and stretched. Yechh. I felt *awful*. No wonder I'd fallen asleep. Maybe I was coming down with something again. Boy, was I thirsty. Did I have a fever? I didn't care. All I knew was that I needed something to drink —

desperately. I was opening my change purse when I remembered that the train didn't have a snack car. *Now* what was I going to do? Well, I don't need to have a soda, I told myself. Water will do just fine.

I looked behind me. Thank goodness there was a bathroom on my car. A bathroom would have running water and little paper cups, wouldn't it?

Sort of. I mean, I was half right. The bathroom, which, by the way, didn't smell so hot, had a sink with nice, cold running water. It even had a bar of dirty pink soap and a stack of paper towels. But there were no cups.

I thought of this silly fold-up plastic cup that Mom used to bring along on vacations — for situations just like this. I used to tease her about that cup. Now I would have *paid* her for it.

I stood in the bathroom and thought. The idea of *not* drinking some water didn't even occur to me. It was just a question of *how* to drink it. Finally I decided that there was only one thing to do. Wrinkling my nose, I washed my hands with the dirty soap. I figured that washing my hands with dirty soap was cleaner than not washing them at all. When I finished, I turned off the hot water, cupped my hands under the cold water, and drank . . . and drank

. . . and drank. Ooh. At that moment, nothing — not even chocolate — would have tasted as good as that water did.

I went back to my seat.

Five minutes later I was thirsty again.

By the time I reached Grand Central Station, I had gotten up for drinks of water six more times. (And I had been to the bathroom twice.) When I saw Dad at the information booth, the first thing I said to him was, "Can I buy a soda?" My thirst was raging. I could not make it go away.

Dad looked closely at me as he took my bag. "Sweetie?" he said. "Are you feeling all right?"

"Not really," I had to admit. I didn't think I could hide it any longer.

"What about dinner?" asked Dad.

"I'm *star*ving," I replied. "I've been starving all day — "

"Have you eaten?" Dad interrupted.

"Yes. Breakfast and lunch." (I didn't mention the package of M&M's that I'd sneaked while I was hiding in the girls' room.) "But I'm still hungry. The only thing is, I'm tired, too. I'd *like* to go out to dinner. I love the Sign of the Dove, but I'm just not sure — I mean, I don't know — "

Dad interrupted me again. "We'll eat at

home. We'll order something in. Let's get a cab right away." He began hurrying toward the doors.

"Can I get a soda first?" I asked.

"Can't you wait until we get home?"

I shook my head.

"All right." Dad looked even more concerned as he glanced around for the nearest concession stand. He bought me a large diet soda. I finished it before we reached his apartment.

That evening Dad ordered two kinds of salad and some sandwiches from a nearby deli. We ate dinner in the kitchen, which was much more relaxing than eating out, even at the Sign of the Dove. I changed into jeans, and Dad and I just sat around and talked and ate.

I considered calling Laine, but by nine o'clock I was *so* relaxed that I yawned and said, "I think I'll go to bed now."

"Now?" Dad looked surprised.

"Yeah, I'm really zonked." Thirsty, too, but I didn't say so.

It was hard to hide this from Dad, though. His apartment is not all that big. There's only one bathroom, and it's closer to his bedroom than to mine. So he heard me when I kept getting up all night for drinks of water. (At least Dad's bathroom has clean soap and my own personal glass.)

Once during the night, Dad was waiting for me when I came out of the bathroom. "Are you okay?" he asked. "I knew we shouldn't have ordered from the deli."

"Oh, my stomach's fine," I answered. "It's just that I'm still so thirsty. I keep drinking water and then I have to go to the bathroom all the time."

Dad frowned. "We should check your blood sugar level."

"*Now?*" It was three-thirty. "No way. I'm falling asleep. Tomorrow." I made my getaway as quickly as I could.

But by the next morning, when I was still drinking like crazy, Dad didn't even suggest checking my blood sugar again. He just said, "I think it's time to call the doctor, don't you?"

I nodded. Something was very wrong. I couldn't deny it any longer.

Dad ran for the phone. When he couldn't reach my doctor immediately, he put me in a cab and we rode to the nearest hospital.

CHAPTER 7

Sunday

Last night I babysat for Charlot Johansin. At first I was worreid that she midgt whant to play martins again but I didn't need to worry about that she never mention martins she whanted to play Memory. That was OK whith me. Beleive it or not I'm am a good memory player so is Charlote so we were evenly matched. It turned out that I shold have been worreid about something else I shold have been worreid about Stacey. But I was'nt so I was pretty surprized to get the phone call form Mrs. McGill.

Saturday had been a good day for Claud. At least that's what she said the first time we had a chance to talk after I was admitted to the hospital. The cab had taken Dad and me to one of New York's finest. However, having been in a number of hospitals, I can tell you that no matter what . . . the food *stinks*. It makes the food in our school cafeteria look — and taste — like gourmet dishes prepared by a great chef of the world. In a hospital nowadays, everything that can be is individually wrapped — a slice of bread in a plastic wrapper, juice in a disposable plastic cup with a foil lid, etc. I would look at my plate after a meal, and it would practically be hidden by a pile of plastic and foil and paper.

What a waste.

If one person in one hospital generates this much trash, I thought, after my first "factory-fresh" meal, how can our environment possibly deal with it? How can — Oops. I am *way* off the track. I'll tell you about the hospital later. What I started to tell you about was Claudia and her good day. It began with a pottery class. At the end of the class, Ms. Baehr, the teacher, chose Claudia's piece (I think Claud said she was working on a vase) as "exemplary" and asked the rest of the class to look at it before they went home. What a boost to Claudia's ego!

That afternoon, Claud studied for a spelling test. When Janine quizzed her on the words, Claud spelled seventeen out of twenty correctly (although you'd never know it from her notebook entry).

And then Claudia headed for the Johanssens'. After such a good day, she wasn't *too* worried that Charlotte would want to be a Martian chef again, but it had crossed her mind after reading my last notebook entry. However, the first thing Charlotte said when her parents left was, "Let's play Memory, Claudia, okay? I have a new Memory game!"

"You do?" said Claudia.

"Yup." Charlotte pulled Claud into the living room. "Here. Sit on the floor," she said. "The game's in my room. I'll go get it."

Charlotte dashed up the stairs and a few moments later reappeared with a box of square cards, which she dumped onto the floor between her and Claudia.

Claud glanced at one of the upturned cards. "This looks different," she commented.

"I told you it was a new game." Charlotte grinned. "See, instead of matching up pairs of things, like two beach balls, you match animal mothers with their babies. A cat with her kitten, a goose with her gosling. Get it?"

"Yup," replied Claud. "This should be fun."

"It is," Char exclaimed. "I beat Mommy twice today."

"Really? That's terrific."

"Thanks. Now let's spread out the cards."

Charlotte and Claudia needed several minutes to mix up the cards, turn them all facedown, and then arrange them on the rug in a neat square of rows.

When that was done, Charlotte said grandly, "You may go first, Claudia. You're a new player, and I've already won some games."

"Okay." Claudia randomly turned over two cards.

"A puppy and a chick. No match!" cried Char.

Claudia turned the two cards facedown again, and then Charlotte took her turn at trying to find a pair. No match.

The game continued. It was very close. Charlotte is just plain smart, and Claudia has a good visual memory. (Maybe that's why art is so appealing to her.)

The game was tied nine to nine when the telephone rang.

"I'll get it!" said Char.

"Okay," replied Claudia. "But remember, don't say that your mommy and daddy aren't at home. Just say — "

"I know," Charlotte interrupted. "Say they can't come to the phone right now. Then take a message."

"Right." Claudia smiled.

"Oh, and no peeking at the cards while I'm gone," said Char.

"Promise," Claud answered. "No peeking. Cross my heart."

Charlotte ran into the kitchen. A few moments later she returned to the living room. "Claudia?" she said, with a catch in her voice. "That's Mrs. McGill. She wants to talk to you. She sounds like she's been crying or something."

"Are you sure?" said Claud, not even bothering to wait for an answer. She dashed into the kitchen and picked up the phone. "Mrs. McGill?" she said.

My mother *did* sound as if she'd been crying. That was because she had been. My father had called her an hour or two earlier, to tell her what had happened. And as soon as they hung up, Mom had freaked out completely. Then she began packing two suitcases — one for her and one for me.

Mom thought about driving straight to New York that very moment, but Dad discouraged her. This was not because he didn't want to see her. It was because she wouldn't have enough time to pack before the last train of the night left for New York, and Dad could tell that Mom was much too worried to drive the car for two hours in the pitch-black. So Mom decided to drive to New York the next morning. (I know all this because Dad was sitting in a chair in my private room at the hospital when he called Mom. I couldn't help but hear his end of the conversation.)

Maybe it was no wonder that Mom had freaked out. She and Dad and I know that with the kind of diabetes I have, I can get sick no matter how strictly I stick to my diet and no matter how careful I am about giving myself the insulin injections. I guess none of us wanted to think about that, though.

Anyway, Mom felt better (she said) if she kept herself busy. So first she packed the suitcases. She knew I'd brought only enough things for the weekend, so she put some extra underwear, some nightgowns, my bathrobe, and a few other things into a bag for me.

Then she reorganized the closet.

And then she called Claudia.

She knew that Claud and the rest of my friends should be told what had happened. *They* would freak out if they thought my mom and I had disappeared off the face of the earth. Anyway, a best friend should know when *her* best friend is in the hospital.

"Hi, Claudia?" said my mother when Claud

61

picked up the phone in the Johanssens' kitchen. Mom wasn't sure how to break the news.

"This is Claudia. Um . . . is everything all right?"

"Well, not exactly. I guess I might as well come right out and tell you. Stacey went into the hospital today. In New York."

"Oh, my lord," Claud whispered. "What happened?" (Claud told me later that the first thing she thought of was *not* my diabetes but the horrible news reports she hears on TV every night. All the murders and attacks and muggings in New York. I don't think this is quite fair, because people can get mugged or murdered anywhere, but I guess New York City *does* have a bad reputation.)

"Stacey's blood sugar has shot way up," my mom told Claud.

At this point, Claud actually sighed with relief. She'd been picturing me lying in bed with stab wounds or something. But then Mom went on to say, "She's pretty sick. The doctors aren't yet sure *why* her blood sugar level is so high. Right now, they're just trying to stabilize it. Then they'll begin doing tests. A lot of them, apparently. She may be in the hospital for awhile. . . . I just thought you'd want to know."

"Oh . . . oh, yes. I — I'm glad you called.

I mean — I mean, I'm sorry Stacey's sick," Claudia stammered, "but I do want to know. . . . Can I call her?"

"Sure. Not tonight, because she needs her rest, but I know she'd be delighted to hear from her friends tomorrow. And if she's still in the hospital next weekend — and I'm not saying she will be — but if she is, you can come visit her on Saturday or Sunday, if your parents give you permission."

"Okay," said Claud, her voice shaking slightly. She took down the phone number that my mom gave her. Then Mom said she was leaving for New York the next day, asked Claud to get my homework assignments from my teachers (why did Mom have to think of *that?*), and told Claud not to worry and that she'd keep in touch.

When Claudia hung up the phone, she knew what she had to do first. Tell Charlotte the news. And she would have to do that carefully, since Charlotte is pretty attached to me.

"Char?" said Claudia, not wasting a moment.

"Yes?" Charlotte had been standing in the doorway to the kitchen all that time. She knew something was wrong.

"Char, um, let's go into the living room and talk." Claudia led Charlotte to the couch and sat down next to her. "I guess the easiest way to tell you this is just to say it. Stacey's in the hospital in New York."

Charlotte looked horrified. "Did the Stalker get her?" she asked shrilly.

"What?" said Claud.

"The Stalker. I've been reading about him in the paper. He stalks girls and then he — "

"Oh, no!" interrupted Claud. "It's not that. Stacey's sick. Her diabetes."

"Oooh."

And in a flash, pretty much as Claudia had expected, Charlotte fell apart. She began to sob. All Claudia could do was hold her. She couldn't tell her it would be all right, because she didn't know that for sure. However, when Char had calmed down, she and Claud put together a care package for me: a crossword puzzle book, a drawing by Charlotte, and a few other things. Claud promised to mail it to me on Monday. During the rest of the evening, Charlotte asked questions such as, "Is Stacey going to die? What if she has to stay in New York where her doctors are and she can never come back here?"

Poor Claudia was stuck with the job of trying to answer those questions — and later with calling the other BSC members to spread the bad news.

CHAPTER 8

On Sunday at noon, Mom walked into my room at the hospital. I had been in there for almost twenty-four hours. Dad had stayed with me the entire time, except for a few hours very early in the morning when he went back to his apartment to try to catch a little sleep and to change his clothes. I had told Dad that he didn't *have* to stay with me, but when he said that he wanted to, I was secretly glad. You won't understand why unless you've been in the hospital yourself. (I mean, apart from the time you were born. That doesn't count, because you don't remember it.) The thing is that no matter how hard the doctors and nurses and other staff members try, most hospitals are very impersonal places. They feel impersonal, anyway. At least to me. I don't care how many clowns come to visit or how many pretty posters and balloons decorate the walls of the ward. A hospital is still a hospital, and that means:

— There are so many nurses and doctors you can't keep track of them all. (I wished my specialist were there, but he was on vacation for two weeks. He wasn't even in New York.)

— You wonder how the nurses and doctors know who *you* are. (Are you really Stacey McGill — a person — or are you just "that patient in Room 322"?)

— You have hardly any privacy. All day long, you are poked and prodded, sometimes by people you've never seen before. All night long, the nurses check on you. This happens about once an hour. Since the door to your room is left open, there is always light flooding in on you. On top of that, squeaky, rubbery nurses' shoes constantly step into your room. Sometimes they approach your bed, and then you know that the night nurse is going to take your temperature or something.

For these reasons and a lot more, I was glad that Dad stayed with me. *Dad* knew I was Stacey McGill, his daughter, a person — and not just "that patient in Room 322." He could be my advocate. Oh, well. I'm off the subject again.

As I started to say before, Mom showed up on Sunday around noon.

"Mom!" I cried when I saw her. (I don't know why I sounded so surprised. She had told Dad, and he had told me, that Mom was going to come to New York that day and stay until I was out of the hospital.)

"Hi, sweetie," Mom replied. Her eyes were bright with tears, but she didn't cry. Instead, she leaned over, kissed me, and placed a big, fuzzy, pink pig next to me. "I tried to find Porky Pig," she said apologetically, "but that's hard to do on short notice." (Porky Pig is a favorite of mine. I can even imitate his voice.)

"That's okay," I said. "I don't think I've ever had a stuffed pig before."

Mom's eyes cleared and she smiled at me.

I smiled back, looking from my mom to my dad and back to my mom again. When was the last time the three of us had been in the same room at the same time? I wasn't sure, but it definitely felt nice. My family was together again.

But not for long.

As soon as Mom had taken off her coat and found a place to sit down, Dad jumped up from his chair. "I could use some coffee," he said. (Or, I *think* that's what he said. He left the room so fast I wasn't sure.)

Mom and I were alone. Before Mom could ask how I was feeling or what the doctors were doing, I said, "I hope my room isn't too messy for you."

Mom looked puzzled. She glanced around her. "You just got here yesterday, Stacey," she said. "You haven't had time to make a mess."

I laughed. "No, I mean my room at Dad's apartment. You probably couldn't even find the bed. I left clothes everywhere. Your suitcase — "

"Honey," Mom interruped me, "I'm not staying in your room. I'm staying at Laine's apartment, in the guest bedroom."

"You're staying at the Cummingses'?" I exclaimed. *"Why?"*

"Because," Mom said calmly, "your aunt and uncle are out of town." (I have some relatives in New York, but I don't see them very often.)

"Why aren't you staying at *Dad's*, though?" I asked.

"Stacey, your father and I are divorced."

"I know you're divorced," I said crankily. "Does that mean you can't stay under the same roof together?"

"In our case, yes," Mom answered.

I think she was going to say something

more, but she changed her mind and stopped speaking. So *I* changed the subject.

"Look at my arm," I said. I held it out. In the crook of my right elbow were two Band-Aids. "They keep drawing blood to do tests on it. And every time I go to the bathroom, I have to go in a plastic cup. They keep testing my urine. It is *so* embarrassing. . . . Have you talked to any of the doctors yet?"

"Not yet," replied Mom. "Your father has, though. And no one knows much more than they did yesterday."

I guess that was why doctors and nurses were bustling in and out of my room more than usual. Not only did they continue to draw blood and to check my urine, but they tested my kidney function. They also raised my insulin. But that didn't seem to make a difference.

"It hasn't made a difference *yet*," Mom reminded me. "But it might."

I nodded. I was worried, though.

When Dad returned an hour and a half later (that was some long coffee break), Mom rushed out just as quickly as my father had earlier, saying that now *she* needed coffee.

"Dad," I said when Mom had left, "you don't have to stay with me."

"I know I don't — " Dad started to say.

"No, really. It's okay," I told him. "I think

I need a nap. I'm pretty tired. Why don't you go home for awhile?"

"We-ell." Dad was hedging.

"I need my address book and some more toothpaste," I told him.

"All right," said Dad.

I was alone. I didn't really need the address book or the toothpaste, but I did need some time to think in private (despite what I'd said earlier about wanting people with me, and hospitals being impersonal and everything). I turned my pillow over, eased myself against it, and started to think about Mom and Dad.

Before I had gotten too far, though, I found myself just gazing around my room. It was like every hospital room I'd ever been in, except that it was private. Sometimes I have stayed in double rooms, or even in rooms with three other kids. Private rooms are much smaller, of course, but then you do have a sense of privacy. (Duh. That's why they're called "private" rooms.) Well, you don't *really* have privacy because of the constant stream of doctors, nurses, nurse's aides, maintenance people, and anyone else who feels that he or she has a job to do in your room. But at least you don't have to put up with other patients and their visitors.

In my room was my bed. (Of course. That's the most important feature of any hospital room.) It was one of those beds that can change position. During the day, I raised the part that's under my top half so that I could sit up. On the bed were sheets and two thin white blankets. I think the same company must provide blankets to every hospital in the world. The sheets, by the way, were stamped with the name of the hospital. I can't imagine why. Did anyone think that a patient would actually want to be reminded of her hospital stay by stashing a set of the sheets in a closet at home? Anyway, apart from my bed were two chairs for visitors, a bed table so that I could eat meals comfortably right in bed, a dresser, and a TV. The TV was bolted into a corner of the room, up near the ceiling. Now why was it bolted? It would be awfully hard to smuggle a television set out of the hospital. I mean, a TV isn't exactly something you can slip into your pocket or hide under your coat. Oh, well. I was glad there was a TV at all, even if it was bolted to the wall at such an angle that I got a stiff neck if I watched it for long.

I looked out the window. The view was of a gray building across the street. I couldn't tell whether it was an office building or some kind of warehouse. Whatever it was, it was boring. But a room with a bad view was better than a room with no view at all. I watched two pigeons swoop by. And, for the first time, began to worry (and I mean heavy-duty worry) about why I was in the hospital. Was it all the candy and sugar I'd eaten recently? Maybe. But I hadn't been feeling well before I'd gone off my diet. I guess the sugar didn't help things, though. How sick was I? Why did I need a change in my insulin? Learning that I'm a brittle diabetic hadn't concerned me too much. As long as the insulin was doing its job, I was okay. But now the insulin wasn't working. What if the doctors raised the level and I got better for awhile, but then needed even *more* insulin? What if no one could find a way to give me *enough* insulin? What if . . . I died? I'd read a book once about a girl with diabetes who couldn't get enough insulin and she *did* die. I also knew that was extremely rare. But what if it happened to me?

Stop playing "what if," I told myself.

I couldn't, though. I felt trapped in my room. Four stark white walls, the dreary building across the street, not even any pigeons now. What if the doctors couldn't find —

"Hey, Stace," said a familiar voice.

I turned my gaze from the window to the doorway. There stood Laine Cummings.

"Hi!" I exlaimed. "Come on in. Have an uncomfortable seat." (The two chairs for visitors were made of hard, molded plastic.)

Laine grinned. She slumped into one of the chairs. "Ah. Restful," she said.

I laughed. "So how did you get in here?"

"Hey, I'm over twelve," replied Laine. "Anyway, at the visitors' desk downstairs I just pretended I was part of this crowd who was going to visit other people. Then I got off on your floor. . . . So how are you feeling?"

"Relieved, I guess," I told her. "Well, not completely relieved. I'm really worried about whatever is wrong with me. But I have to admit that now that I'm in the hospital, awful as it is, I'm glad to know there are all these doctors around. I feel taken care of."

"That's good," said Laine slowly. She frowned slightly. Then her face brightened. "Wait till you see what I brought you!" she cried.

"What?" I asked suspiciously. Laine's taste can sometimes be strange. Once, she had given me a key chain that looked like a cicada (a really ugly, *big*, green, winged bug). That was bad enough. But when you pressed a button on the underside of the bug, its green eyes flashed on and off, and it made this weird high-pitched humming sound. (I scared people with it until the battery wore out.)

"Okay," said Laine. "First" (she reached into a plastic bag that she'd set on the floor beside her chair), "these beautiful flowers.

Anyone who goes to the hospital should receive flowers. So here you are." Laine handed me a bouquet of electric-blue plastic tulips. They were packaged beautifully in Handi-Wrap.

"Charming," I said. I stuck them in an empty water pitcher.

"And they're low-maintenance," Laine went on. "No watering, and they don't need any light. Just dust them once in awhile."

I giggled. "Okay."

"Next," said Laine, reaching into the bag again, "is this." She handed me a small box. "It came from the Last Wound-Up."

"Oh, goody!" I cried. (The Last Wound-Up is this store near Laine's apartment that sells all sorts of funny wind-up toys.) I lifted the lid. Inside the box lay a huge brown plastic spider — wearing a pair of red glasses. Laine wound him up and let him wiggle across my bed table.

"Gross!" I exclaimed. But I couldn't help laughing.

"Can you believe it?" Laine said. "I got the red glasses somewhere else. They just happend to fit the spider."

"He looks very scholarly," I told Laine.

Laine and I watched the spider crawl across the table and fall to the floor.

"Two more things," Laine continued. She

handed me a big, gaudy get-well card.

"Thanks!" I said.

"And last," began Laine, "I talked with the members of the BSC. I called Claudia this morning, and it turned out that your friends were holding an emergency club meeting. I have messages from everybody. Mal says she's thinking about you. Mary Anne and Dawn say they miss you. Kristy says to get back on your feet because Dawn isn't all that good at handling the money in the treasury. Jessi promises to write to you so you'll be sure to get mail in the hospital. And Claud says she's getting your homework assignments — and that she misses you an awful lot."

By the time Laine left, I felt very cheered up.

CHAPTER 9

Wednesday morning.

I was beginning my fourth full day of hospital life. My blood sugar level had been lowered, but the doctors still weren't satisfied. They were giving me an awful lot of insulin just to keep the blood sugar *down* — but not where it should be. However, I was feeling better. I was much less tired. Mom encouraged me to make my days as normal as possible.

That meant getting dressed, doing homework assignments (plus *still* trying to catch up in most of my subjects), and waking up fairly early. No sleeping late. (Darn it.) Of course, it would have been difficult to sleep late anyway, considering the bustle of hospital life. What was a typical day like for me? Well, I'll tell you.

Wednesday began at seven o'clock when my alarm clock (yes, my alarm clock) went off. I got up, changed out of my nightgown and into regular old street clothes (jeans and stuff), and washed up as well as I could in my bathroom. (The bathroom had a sink and a toilet, but no shower or tub.)

At seven-thirty I flopped onto my bed and began doing schoolwork. My mom had said that getting dressed and leading a "normal" life would make my hospital stay more manageable. And it did, I guess. Even so, the hospital was still a foreign place, with lots of intrusions on my "normalcy."

For instance, by eight o'clock, I was deeply engrossed in writing an overdue essay for social studies, when I heard carts and machinery being rolled down the hall. "Yuck," I said to myself. "It's — "

"Time for vital signs," said a nurse cheerfully as he wheeled a blood pressure instrument into my room. (I happen to know that the blood pressure instrument is called a sphygmomanometer. This is the kind of information you pick up when you spend a lot of time in hospitals and doctors' offices.)

"Okay," I replied. I put my books aside. Then I sat in one of the visitor's chairs and, without being told, opened my mouth and extended my arm.

The nurse grinned. "I guess you're an old pro now," he said.

"Unfortunately," I agreed.

The nurse put a thermometer in my mouth and wrapped the black cuff of the sphygmo-manometer around my upper arm. He listened to the pulse in the crook of my elbow with a stethoscope for a few moments, made a note on a chart, and then said, "Stand, please." I stood. I don't know why they take your blood pressure when you're both sitting and stand-ing, but they do.

I sat down again. The nurse removed the cuff from my arm. Then he took my pulse. Just as he was finishing, the thermometer beeped. I should add here that the thermom-eter wasn't a regular glass one. It was plastic and wired to a box. A tone sounded when the thermometer was done taking your tempera-ture, and then your temperature flashed up digitally on the box, like the time on a clock radio. Another miracle of modern medicine.

"All systems go," said the nurse.

"Good," I replied. Then I added, "Thank you."

The nurse's name was Rufus. (That's what was printed across the front of his uniform.) But I didn't bother to remember it. A different nurse had taken my vital signs every morning.

I returned to my social studies essay, only to be interrupted by a nurse's aide bringing breakfast. So I set aside my books and tried to force down the disgusting food. Before I had finished, Mom appeared in the doorway.

"Hi, lovey," she said, settling into a chair.

"Hi!" I answered.

"How are you feeling today?"

"Not bad," I replied. "But I know the doctors are going to fiddle around with the insulin again."

"Well, that's what you're here for."

"I guess."

"Have you been working already?"

I held up the paper with my half-finished essay on it. "I'm trying," I told Mom, "but I keep getting interrupted. Vital signs and breakfast."

"And me."

"No, not you," I said, but I saw that Mom was smiling. She wasn't serious. "Is Dad coming today?" I asked her. (Monday and Tuesday had been somewhat unnerving with Mom and Dad trying to see me but at the same time trying to avoid each other.)

"I don't think so," Mom answered. "I mean, not until later. He has a full day of meetings. I'll stay with you, though."

"Only if you want to," I told her. "Don't feel you have to sit in that chair all day. I have homework, and anyway, I'm much better."

"Okay." Mom actually did leave for awhile. She said she was going to have a cup of coffee somewhere and then take a cab to midtown (where most of my favorite stores are located). She said she was on a secret mission. I hoped it involved clothes shopping — for me.

Mom left as the nurse's aide came to retrieve my tray. I picked up my essay again, and *again* I was interrupted, this time by a whole group of people in long white coats. I recognized only one of them. He was a doctor who'd examined me several times. He began talking, and the rest of the people took notes on clipboards they were carrying. I guessed that they were medical students or new doctors or something, and that my doctor was their teacher.

The doctor greeted me, then turned back to his class. "This patient," he said, "is a thirteen-year-old girl" (he didn't even use my name!) "with juvenile onset of diabetes. She was hospitalized last Saturday, at which time she was found to have an abnormally high blood sugar level, despite the fact that she's been taking insulin and has been on a strict diet since she was first diagnosed. . . ."

The doctor went on and on, and the students scribbled away on their clipboards and sometimes glanced at me. I felt like a fish in a glass bowl or an animal in a cage at the zoo. The doctor talked about me as if I weren't sitting just three feet away from him.

Anyway, the group left my room after five

minutes or so. Once *again*, I settled down to work. And this time I was able to accomplish a few things even though a nurse came to check my blood, and even though I knew *Jeopardy* was on TV, followed by a rerun of *The Beverly Hillbillies*. After a bland, tasteless lunch, I worked some more. Then Mom reappeared with a Benetton bag. (Yea!) In it was a beautiful emerald-green sweater and a matching beret.

"Oh, thank you!" I cried. I tried on the new things immediately. Mom stayed with me until about four-thirty. Then she said she had to leave. I think she was afraid she'd run into my father, since she wasn't sure when he was going to show up that day.

By 4:45, I was alone.

At 5:00, the telephone rang. I reached over to pick it up.

"Hello?" I said. "This is the funny farm. To whom are you speaking?"

There was a pause. Then a giggly voice said, "I'm speaking to *you!*"

It was Claud. Even so, I said, "Oh. Well, who's this?"

"It's me! Claudia!"

"I know that," I replied. We were both laughing by then.

"How are you doing?" Claud wanted to know.

"Okay," I answered. "I feel a lot better, but I might have to stay here awhile."

I knew Claud wanted to ask, "Why?" I also knew that she could tell I didn't feel like talking about whatever was wrong with me. So after a brief, uncomfortable pause, Claudia said, "The rest of the club is here. Everyone wants to say hi."

"The rest of the club is there?" I repeated. "It's only five o'clock."

"I know. We all wanted to talk to you, so we met early."

"Hey, how are you guys going to pay for this phone call?" I asked suspiciously. "It's going to be an expensive one."

"With treasury money?" Claudia replied.

I sighed. Then I said, "Well, I guess I'm worth it."

Claud laughed. She put Kristy on the phone. Kristy announced that Emily Michelle had learned a new word: stinky. Only she pronounced it "tinky." *Every*thing was tinky, according to Emily.

I talked to the rest of my friends. When Jessi got on the phone, I asked her how Charlotte Johanssen was doing.

"She's . . . fine," Jessi replied, and quickly handed the phone to Mallory.

By the time we hung up, it was nearly five-thirty. We were all talked out, and I was worried that the cost of a few more half-hour, long-distance phone calls would wipe out the treasury. Oh, well. I needed my friends. I could tackle the treasury problem when I returned to Stoneybrook.

Just as I was putting the phone back in its cradle, Laine showed up. But we barely had a chance to say hello when a package was brought into my room by a hospital aide. (You never know when you are going to get mail at the hospital. It seems to appear whenever it pleases.)

"A package!" said Laine. "Cool. Who's it from?"

I checked the return address. "Hey, it's from Charlotte!"

I ripped the brown paper off the box, then lifted its lid. The lid was labeled CARE PACKAGE. Inside I found the things that Claud and Charlotte had put together on the evening of my first day in the hospital.

"I think I'll call Char," I told Laine. I was remembering Jessi's response when I'd asked her how Charlotte was doing. Was something wrong?

I soon found out. Char was ecstatic to hear from me. At first. But soon her excitement changed to a series of questions, each one more anxious than the first. When was I going to get out of the hospital? When would I come back to Stoneybrook? I *was* coming back to Stoneybrook, wasn't I? Why hadn't my insulin shots been working? Did I *really* feel better, or was I just saying so to be polite? Char's last question was, "Do people die from diabetes?" (I'm pretty sure she meant was *I* going to die?) But before I could answer her, she said, "Oh, that's okay. Never mind, Stacey. I'll ask my mom. She'll know the answer."

Gently, I turned the topic of conversation to the care package. But when I hung up the phone, I said to Laine, "I think I've got a problem with Charlotte."

CHAPTER 10

Friday

Stacey was right. Well, she was half right. There was a problem with Charlotte. But it wasn't just Stacey's problem. We all had to deal with it. It was a good thing that the day after her talk with Char, Stacey called Claud to tell her what was going on. This was good because Claudia called me, knowing that I was going to sit for Charlotte last night. I went to the Johanssens' prepared for trouble. It wasn't major trouble -- like sitting at the Rodowskys' for Jackie, the walking disaster. Still, it worried me, so I talked to Dr. and Mr. Johanssen when *they came home from their meeting. They're worried, too, but they think the only solution is to wait. To wait for Stacey to come home, all well, so that Charlotte can see that everything is okay.*

Dawn hasn't baby-sat at the Johanssens' as much as some of the other members of the BSC have, but she knows plenty about Charlotte from listening to us (especially me) talk about her, and from reading the club notebook. Also, as she wrote in her own notebook entry, I called Claud after my conversation with Charlotte, and Claudia called Dawn. Dawn, knowing how attached Charlotte is to me, immediately understood that Char might be overly concerned about my health. She might be weepy or clingy.

Dawn was not, however, expecting to find that Char had become a hypochondriac, even though the Johanssens themselves warned her about it.

"I actually kept her home from school two days this week," Dr. Johanssen told Dawn. Dawn had rung the bell a few moments earlier. She had expected Charlotte to answer the door, but she was nowhere in sight. Dr. Johanssen had answered the door instead, and now she, Dawn, and Charlotte's father were holding a whispered conversation in the front hall.

"But she's not sick?" Dawn said.

"I don't think so. One day she said she had a sore throat. The next day she said her stomach hurt. Now she's complaining of a headache and an earache. She hasn't had a fever, and her appetite — even on the day she stayed home with the stomachache — has been just fine."

"Okay," said Dawn slowly. "In case she *is* sick, I'll keep her quiet tonight."

"That won't be hard," said Mr. Johanssen with a smile. "She's upstairs in bed. I think she plans to stay there." The Johanssens left a few minutes later. Dawn headed upstairs with her Kid-Kit.

"Charlotte?" Dawn ventured, as she reached the doorway to her bedroom.

"Hi, Dawn," replied Char.

It was only seven-thirty, and already Charlotte was wearing her nightgown. However, she was not actually *in* bed. She was sitting on the covers, looking through a book.

"How are you feeling?" asked Dawn.

Charlotte paused. Then she replied, "My neck hurts."

"Your neck? I thought your mom said you have a headache and an earache."

"I do. I mean, I did," Char answered. "But now my neck hurts."

"Are your headache and earache gone, or do you still have them *plus* the problem with your neck?" Dawn asked.

"I think they're gone. It's really just my neck. . . . I hope I don't have a pinched nerve in my spine."

"A pinched nerve!" exclaimed Dawn. "How do you know about pinched nerves?"

"I know about a lot of things. Mommy's a doctor," Charlotte reminded Dawn.

"Oh," said Dawn. She sat on the edge of Charlotte's bed. "Well, if you have a pinched nerve, how do you think it got that way?"

Charlotte shrugged. "I don't know. But I'm pretty sure that's what it is. I should tell Mommy. I should be wearing one of those neck braces. And if the brace doesn't work, then I might need an operation . . . in the hospital."

"Well, for now," said Dawn, "why don't you just try to hold your head still."

"Okay," Charlotte answered uncertainly.

"So what do you want to do tonight? Have you finished your homework already?"

"Yes," said Charlotte. "Only I don't think

it matters. I probably won't be in school to-morrow. You know."

"Yeah. What with the pinched nerve and all." Dawn hoisted the Kid-Kit onto the bed. "We'll do something quiet tonight."

"Good. I better not overexert myself."

"You better not *what?*"

"Overexert myself," Charlotte repeated. "That means that I — "

"I know what it means," Dawn interrupted. "I'm just a little surprised that *you* know what it means."

"It's something my mom says sometimes," Char informed Dawn. From the Kid-Kit she had pulled a copy of an old-looking book called *The Dachshunds of Mama Island*. "What's this?" she asked.

"Oh. That used to belong to my mother," said Dawn. "She found it and gave it to me. The story is a little old-fashioned, but I think you'd like it."

"Okay. Let's read," said Charlotte.

Dawn opened the book, being careful of its tattered dust jacket. She began to read to Charlotte, who seemed interested in the story right away. After about ten minutes, though, Charlotte said, "Dawn? I don't feel too good."

"Your neck?" asked Dawn. "Why don't you lie down then."

Charlotte shook her head. "It isn't my neck. It's my stomach. It's sort of aching and burning. I think maybe I have an ulcer."

Dawn tried to come up with an appropriate response. Finally she said, "People your age hardly ever get ulcers. If you have one, it's pretty rare. What did you eat for dinner tonight?"

"Dawn, this is not indigestion," said Charlotte indignantly.

"All right. How bad is the burning?"

"Why?" asked Charlotte warily.

"Because I'm thinking that maybe I should call your parents to see if I can give you some Mylanta or Pepto-Bismol or something."

"Oh, no," said Char quickly. "You don't have to do that. But — but now I'm all tired and *really* thirsty. Do you think I have diabetes . . . like Stacey?"

What *was* this? Dawn asked herself. Sore throats, pinched nerves, ulcers, diabetes. She didn't think Charlotte was sick at all. But how could she convince Charlotte of that?

Then Dawn got an idea. "No, I don't think you have diabetes," she said quickly. "Listen, Char, do you still have your old doctor's kit?"

"Sure. It's in my toy chest."

Dawn located the black plastic bag and set it on Char's bed. "I better give you a checkup," she said. "I should find out what's wrong with you before I interrupt your parents at their meeting."

"But — " Char started to say.

"No buts," replied Dawn. "Hold still. I have to listen to your heart."

Dawn held the plastic stethoscope to Char's chest. She stuck a fake thermometer under her tongue. She used every instrument that was in the kit. She even wore the pair of red, glassless glasses. "You're perfectly healthy," she announced several minutes later.

"Can I talk now?" asked Char.

"Yup."

"Dawn, that is a *toy* doctor's kit. And anyway, you aren't a doctor."

Dawn sighed. "Shall we read some more?" she asked.

"Okay. Even though I really do think I have diabetes. I may be anemic, too."

Dawn spent the next hour trying to convince Charlotte that she wasn't sick. Nothing worked. At last she told Char that a patient needs plenty of sleep, so she put her to bed. Dawn tiptoed downstairs with her Kid-Kit and worked on a school assignment until the Johanssens returned.

"How was Charlotte?" asked Mr. Johanssen.

"Fine," Dawn replied, gathering up her books and papers, "except that she now thinks she has a pinched nerve in her spine, an ulcer, diabetes, and possibly anemia."

Dr. and Mr. Johanssen exchanged a glance. "Hmm," said Char's mother.

"I hope I handled everything okay," said Dawn. She explained what she'd done.

"That sounds fine," Dr. Johanssen replied.

"Um . . . can I ask a question?" said Dawn.

"Of course."

"Why do you think Charlotte is acting this way? It must have something to do with Stacey, but I don't know what."

"We're not sure ourselves," said Dr. Johanssen. "But I can guess. Charlotte misses Stacey an awful lot. She wants to see her. I have a feeling that somehow Charlotte thinks — although she's probably not aware of it — that if she gets sick enough, she'll wind up in the hospital with Stacey. Then she can spend time with her, and also reassure herself that Stacey is all right and that she really will come back to Stoneybrook."

"Wow," said Dawn. "What are you going to do?"

"We've been thinking about that," said Mr. Johanssen. "We've just decided to be extra patient and understanding with Charlotte. And to let her be in touch with Stacey as often as she likes."

"All right," replied Dawn. But she was worried.

CHAPTER 11

On Friday morning, my first thought as I woke up was, Oh, no. It's back.

What's back? I asked myself, and realized that I didn't have an answer. I just knew that, although I was still lying in bed (I hadn't even sat up yet), and although I'd slept for almost nine hours, I felt incredibly tired — as if I couldn't move a muscle.

Impatiently, I slapped at my alarm clock. When it stopped ringing, I glared at it. "I don't like you this morning," I told the clock. "And I will not obey you. I am not going to get up."

Actually, I thought, I couldn't get up. I didn't want to admit this to myself, but . . . I . . . felt . . . rotten. The idea of getting dressed and doing schoolwork seemed beyond reason.

I rang for a nurse. Five minutes later, one hurried into my room, pausing briefly to check the nameplate outside my door. She didn't even know who I was. And I wished desperately to be with someone who knew me.

I was scared.

I read the nurse's name tag. Darlene Desmond. A movie-star name.

Okay, so now we each knew the other's name.

"Stacey?" said Ms. Desmond.

I couldn't tell whether that was her way of asking what was wrong, or whether she wanted to make sure that I really was Stacey McGill, as the nameplate said. Oh, well. What did it matter?

"I don't feel too good," I told the nurse. "For the past few days I was feeling a lot better. But now . . . I don't think I can even get out of bed."

That was bad enough. But when Darlene Desmond asked if I needed to go to the bathroom and I said yes, she brought me a *bedpan*. A freezing cold, embarrassing bedpan.

And she stayed with me while I used it.

After I was finished, I said, "I'm supposed to get up, get dressed, and start my homework." But even as I said that, my eyelids were drooping.

"Not this morning," replied the nurse. "You can go back to sleep. I'll talk to your doctor as soon as I can."

"I don't have a doctor," I mumbled. "I have three million of them." But either the nurse

94

was already gone, or I just dreamed those words. At any rate, no reply came.

I fell fast asleep. I slept right through Vital Signs.

I didn't wake up until the carts carrying the breakfast trays began to rattle up and down the hallway. Usually, I enjoy meals. They're never any good, but at least they're a distraction. That morning, though, I had no appetite. I pushed the bed table away and leaned against my pillows. I wasn't tired enough to go back to sleep, but I didn't have the energy to do anything — even to turn on the television.

So when Mom arrived a little while later, that was how she found me; just lying in bed in a quiet room, my uneaten breakfast sitting on the table.

"Are you okay?" Mom asked before she even took off her coat.

"Not really," I replied. I hate seeming weak around my parents, but just then I was too worried to care.

"What's wrong, Stacey?" Mom's face was the picture of alarm.

"I don't know. I feel almost as bad as I did last Saturday."

"I'll go find a doctor," said Mom quickly.

"No, don't. I mean, you don't have to. This

nurse — her name was Ruby Diamond or something — said she'd get a doctor for me."

"How long ago was that?" Mom wanted to know.

"I'm not sure. I fell asleep. She came in right after my alarm clock rang. What time is it now?"

"Nine," my mother replied. "The doctor should already have been here."

She stood up, looking furious, just as a man named Dr. Motz strode into my room. I tried to remember if I'd seen him before.

I decided that I must have, because he greeted me with, "Good morning, Stacey. Good morning, Mrs. McGill. Stacey, one of the nurses said you aren't feeling so hot this morning. Can you tell me what's wrong?"

I almost said, *"You're* supposed to tell *me* what's wrong." But I knew what he meant. Besides, Mom was in the room. So I described how I was feeling. The doctor looked slightly concerned, but all he did was raise my insulin dosage (again) and send in a stream of people to draw my blood and perform other tests, some of which had been performed once or twice earlier in the week. Before Dr. Motz left he said, "Take it easy, Stacey. I'll look in on you again this afternoon or this evening. And I'll let you know the test results as soon as possible."

"Okay," I replied. "See you later."

And Mom called after him, "Thank you!"

Mom and I were alone again. We'd spent a lot of time together that week, just the two of us. Usually, I was working and Mom was reading. But that morning Mom said, "Do you want me to turn on the TV, honey?"

I shook my head. "No. Not now, anyway. . . . Mom?"

"Yes?"

"Is Dad going to visit me today?"

Mom couldn't quite look at me. "Maybe after dinner," she said.

"Why doesn't he come during the day?" I wanted to know. "He's hardly been here at all, ever since . . . " I realized that he'd hardly been there at all ever since my mother had arrived. But I didn't want to say that. It would hurt her feelings. "Ever since, um, Sunday," I finished up.

"You know your father's a workaholic," said Mom, still not looking directly at me.

"Yeah. But couldn't he visit me during his lunch hour? Or on his way to the office in the morning?"

"I suppose. Well, maybe something deeper is going on."

"Such as what?" I asked suspiciously.

"Stacey, your father loves you very much — "

"It doesn't feel like it right now."

"He loves you so much," Mom went on, "that I think it's been very difficult for him to visit you in the hospital. He doesn't like to see you this way."

"Well, I can't help how I look or what happened. If Dad's staying away from me because I'm sick, then he's being very selfish."

At last Mom's gaze met my own. I knew I'd gone one step too far. "That's unfair, Stacey," she said in measured tones. "Listen to me. Do you want to know why your father hasn't been around to see you very often? It's partly because of the things I said, but mostly it's because of me."

"You?"

Mom nodded. "Well, Dad and me. We're having a hard time being together right now. So since I could take time off from my job, and your father can't, we agreed that I would stay with you during the day as much as possible, and he would visit you later."

"Oh." Was that true? Could my parents *really* not be in the same room together for a half an hour or so? Maybe *that* was what was bothering me; not so much that Dad was only spending a little time with me, but that my parents couldn't be together so that the three of us could seem like a family again — at least while I was sick.

"Maybe you should turn on the TV after all," I said to Mom. I didn't want to continue our conversation, but I couldn't just lie in bed while Mom sat next to me, both of us shrouded in silence.

Mom switched the set on and, after changing channels for awhile, we discovered an old Woody Allen movie. We began to laugh. By the time the movie had ended, our argument was forgotten. Well, maybe not forgotten, but over.

At 3:15 that afternoon, Laine showed up. For the past three days, she'd come by to see me as soon as school let out.

I know she was surprised to find me in bed in my nightgown, my hair uncombed. She couldn't hide her surprise. But Mom and I tactfully ignored it, and then my mother excused herself to get a cup of coffee so that Laine and I could spend an hour or two alone together.

"So?" Laine said, sitting down.

"So I'm not feeling too great today." I thought I owed her an explanation.

"Maybe you'll feel better tomorrow," Laine replied with that tone of false cheer that I've heard too often whenever I've been in the hospital.

"Maybe," I echoed.

Laine leaned down and reached into a shopping bag. "I brought you something."

"Again?" I couldn't help smiling. Every time Laine came to visit me, she brought one or two weird things. My room was filling up quickly — with a camouflage-print hat that said "Daddy's Little Hunting Buddy" across the top, a pair of light-up sunglasses, glow-in-the-dark jewelry, a pen that looked like a palm tree, and more.

Laine handed me a box. "Open it," she said.

I lifted the top off. Inside lay a hand mirror. An ordinary, plastic mirror. I had mentioned that I wished I had a mirror in my room, but I was surprised to see such a tame gift from Laine.

"Hold it up," Laine instructed me.

I lifted it in front of my face — and the mirror began to laugh at me!

So did Laine. "Can you believe I found that?" she asked, trying to calm down. "It came from the same place that carries those cicada key rings."

I laughed helplessly, and Laine started up again. We spent the next two hours encouraging anyone who entered my room to look in the mirror.

This one nurse practically fainted.

By the time Laine and my mom had left and

I was waiting for Dad to arrive, I felt better —
emotionally, anyway.

But that didn't last long. Dr. Motz came back
just as my supper was being placed in front
of me.

"Stacey," he said gravely, "tomorrow we
plan to start a new procedure with you. I'll
need to talk to your parents first, but I'm sure
they'll okay it."

"What are you going to do?" I couldn't keep
my voice from trembling.

"Just hook you up to an I.V. for awhile. I
want to see how you do with insulin dripping
constantly into your veins."

"Goody," I said.

When Dr. Motz left, I began to cry.

CHAPTER 12

"There she is!"

"No, that's not her."

"It says 'Stacey McGill' by her door, you dweeb."

Was I dreaming? It was Saturday, I was pretty sure of that. I was also sure that I'd been awakened around eleven-thirty the night before when a nurse hooked me up to the I.V. Then I'd fallen asleep again and had all these weird dreams. Now I could have sworn I heard the voices of my Stoneybrook friends. But that couldn't be true. Why would they be in New York?

"Oh, my lord!" someone cried. "She's got a needle stuck in her arm!"

"SHHH!" said someone else.

"She's sleeping," a whispered voice added.

"No, I'm not." I struggled to open my eyes — and found myself facing Claudia,

102

Dawn, Mary Anne, and Kristy! "Are you really here?" I asked.

"We really are," said Claud.

My head cleared as the four BSC members crowded into my room, hugged me awkwardly (since I was lying down), and dropped presents and packages all over the bed. My friends were beaming.

"We took the train down early this morning," Dawn informed me.

"And we didn't get lost in Grand Central Station," added Mary Anne.

"Jessi and Mal wanted to come, too, but their parents wouldn't let them," said Claudia. "They sent some things for you, though. And Jessi hopes you got the letter she mailed."

"Oh, wow! I can't believe this!" I exclaimed. "I thought I was dreaming. But this is a dream come true."

"Boy, the hospital sure has made you maudlin," said Kristy. She held up one hand and rubbed her index finger back and forth across the top of her thumb.

"What's that?" everyone asked.

"The world's saddest story played on the smallest violin."

I giggled. If I'd had the energy, I would have thrown a pillow at Kristy. Instead, I raised the bed so that I could sit up. I looked at the stuff strewn over my covers.

"You guys are going to spoil me," I said. "What on earth did you bring?"

"Lots of things," replied Claud. "But before you look at them, tell us how you're feeling. You, um, don't sound as good as when I talked to you on Thursday."

"I don't feel as good as I did then." I held up my arm. "They're dripping insulin directly into my veins now. Maybe that will make a difference."

"Gosh," said Mary Anne slowly.

"Let's not talk about it, though," I went on. "I want to know how you guys are doing, and what's been happening in Stoneybrook."

"Okay," replied Claud. She was perched on my bed, Dawn next to her. Kristy and Mary Anne were seated in the chairs.

"Wait," said Kristy. "Before you start, Claud, let me try to make myself even more comfortable than I am right now. This chair is really incredible. I've never felt anything quite like it." Kristy tried to adjust herself so that her spine and shoulder blades weren't mashed up against the back of the hard chair. It was impossible. "Ah. I think I'd like a set of these for my bedroom," added Kristy.

The rest of us were laughing, and I said, "Sorry about that. If you want a padded chair, you have to leave the hospital."

"Are you guys finished?" asked Claud. "I

104

want to tell Stacey what's going on."

We tried to compose ourselves. "Okay. Go ahead," I said.

"Well," Claud began. "First of all, *every*one misses you. When you open some of these cards, you'll be surprised to see who they're from. People are always asking about you, wondering when you'll be back home."

"Like who?" I wanted to know.

"Like *every*one. The Newtons, especially Jamie; the Perkinses, especially Myriah and Gabbie; kids at school, including . . . *Ross Brown*; Mr. — "

"Ross Brown?" I interrupted. (I had this incredible crush on him.) "Does he know I like him?"

Claudia shrugged. Then she grinned and said, "*He* likes *you*."

Wow. . . .

"Mallory's been collecting the mail for you and your mom," spoke up Mary Anne. Then she interrupted herself by saying, "My, these chairs *are* comfy." (We laughed.) "Anyway, yesterday she gave me the interesting-looking stuff. That's here along with everything else."

"Great," I replied. "So what's going on at school?"

"Let's see," Dawn answered. "Alan Gray got suspended for setting off a cherry bomb in the boys' room on the second floor."

"Gross," I said.

"And Cokie got a nose job."

"What?" I cried. "You're kidding!"

"Nope. That's why she's been absent."

"So what does she look like?"

"Like she got a nose job," said Kristy. "You can always tell."

"That's funny. You never noticed *my* nose job," I said.

Kristy turned pale. "*Your* nose job?" she whispered.

"Just kidding," I said.

There was a moment of silence. Then we all began to laugh again. We laughed so loudly I was afraid a nurse would come in and kick my friends out. But nothing happened.

"Okay, open your stuff," Claudia finally managed to say. "Open the cards first. Then open the packages."

"Yes, Mommy," I answered obediently. I picked up the envelope lying nearest to me and slit it open. Inside was a get well card, handmade by five-year-old Claire Pike. GET WELL SON it read, which made us giggle.

"Mallory warned me that the card was a little off. Claire didn't want any help with it," said Dawn.

"I like it the way it is," I announced. " 'Get well, son.' " (More laughter.)

I opened up card after card. In the middle

of this, a nurse came into my room (not Desma Diamond or whoever that other nurse was). She drew some blood, and then she left quickly. She didn't say anything about my having four visitors, which is not allowed. This was because Claud and Dawn were hiding in the bathroom.

"The coast is clear," I called, as soon as the nurse and my blood sample were gone.

Dawn and Claudia returned to the bed. I continued opening cards. I had never seen so many! There were homemade ones from some of the kids I sit for, and store-bought ones from the kids at school, the parents of some of my baby-sitting charges, and even three of my teachers.

"Now for the presents!" cried Claud.

"No, wait," said Mary Anne. "You're forgetting. Remember what's — " She pointed to the hallway beyond my door.

"Oh, yeah," said Claudia. She dashed out of my room and returned carrying the world's largest get-well card. It was at least two feet by three feet.

I felt relieved. I was a bit dizzy, and just the thought of opening the presents made me feel more tired than ever. I also felt sort of clammy. And shaky. It was weird. But I tried to hide this. I didn't want to scare my friends.

"Whoa!" I exclaimed, looking at the card

that was so big it blocked my view of Claud. "Who's that from?"

"Everybody," answered Kristy.

And it was. The card had been signed by parents, teachers, kids, my friends' brothers and sisters, and of course, my friends themselves.

I was exclaiming over the card when that same nurse burst into my room again. She appeared so quickly that Dawn and Claudia didn't have time to duck into the bathroom.

Uh-oh, I thought. Now I'm in for it. I've broken the sacred two-visitor rule.

But the nurse barely noticed my friends. She bustled to one side of my bed and abruptly turned off the I.V. drip, although she did not remove the needle from my arm.

"What are you *doing*?" I cried.

"Your blood sugar level is dropping," the nurse replied. "Doctor Motz will be here any second. And your mom's on her way up from the cafeteria."

As the words were coming out of her mouth, I heard a voice on the intercom system paging Dr. Motz.

Claud and Dawn stood up. So did Kristy and Mary Anne. They backed away from the bed and huddled near the doorway.

Nobody, except the nurse, said a word.

Just a few seconds after the I.V. drip had been stopped, Mom raced into my room. She had beaten Dr. Motz. "Hi, girls," said Mom as she whisked by my friends. Then she did a double take. "Where did *you* come from?" she asked. But she didn't wait for an answer. Instead she began whispering with the nurse.

I felt a cold wave wash over my body and settle in the pit of my stomach, where it sat like a block of ice. I knew something was wrong. Again.

Dr. Motz ran into my room then. He took one look at my friends and said, "Okay. Everybody out. Right now."

"Everybody out?" echoed Claudia.

"On the double," said Dr. Motz, not bothering to look at Claud. He began examining me and talking to the nurse.

"We'll see you later," called Claudia in a trembly voice.

"Yeah, we'll wait outside until they let us come back," added Kristy.

"Okay. And thanks for all the cards and . . ." My voice trailed off because my friends had disappeared, wanting to escape Dr. Motz, I guess. But I had seen something awful on their faces: fear.

They were afraid for me.

So was I.

* * *

By the evening, however, I felt better. Also more optimistic. After a day of testing and consulting, Dr. Motz had come up with a new solution to my insulin problem. I was to start injecting myself with a mixture of the kind of insulin I'd been using before plus a second kind of insulin that I had not used before.

And now that my blood sugar level was more normal, I had some energy and was hardly dizzy at all. I had even eaten dinner.

"Mom?" I said when the frantic pace of the day had slowed down and just my mother and I were left in my room. "Can my friends come back now?"

"Oh, honey, I'm sorry," Mom replied. "They finally had to leave. Their parents wanted them home by six o'clock."

I didn't answer her. I stared out the window.

"Claudia said to be sure to tell you to open your cards and presents as soon as you feel like it. She said she's sorry they had to leave, but that they'll call you tomorrow or on Monday before the club meeting."

"Monday . . . I thought I'd be out of here by Monday," I said.

"Well . . ." Mom replied helplessly. And then she began to put on her coat. "Your father will be here any minute."

110

Was he working today, on a Saturday? I wondered. But what I said was, "Mom, can't you stay here until Dad comes? I want the three of us to be a family again. Even if it's only for five minutes."

"Stacey — " Mom said.

"I'm sorry," I interrupted her. "I understand that this is a bad time for you and Dad, but if we could all be together for awhile, then . . . well, it's really important to me. *Really* important."

I knew I wasn't playing fair. I knew that I was pressuring Mom because I was sick, and that she would give in because she felt guilty. But she did give in. She removed her coat and sat down again.

"This evening may not be what you're hoping for," she warned me.

"Yes, it will. It'll be wonderful." I couldn't believe Mom was staying! "Maybe we can watch TV together, or — "

I stopped talking. Mom wasn't listening to me. She was looking at the doorway.

My father had arrived.

CHAPTER 13

"Stacey!" Dad exclaimed. He strode across the room to my bed and gave me a big hug. "How are you feeling? I'm glad you're off the I.V."

"I'm fine," I replied. "Well, better anyway." Since Dad had not spoken to my mother, I added, "Um, Dad, Mom is still here. She's going to stay for awhile."

"Well, I could use some coffee," my father said.

"No, don't go!" I cried. "Stay here with me. I want to see you guys together again." (What I meant was, "I want to get you guys together again.")

"All right," said Dad. He moved the vacant chair as far from Mom as possible — clear to the opposite side of my bed.

That's something, I thought. He isn't leaving. It's a start.

But that's all it turned out to be. A start.

The rest of the evening was a disaster. Looking back, I don't know whose fault it was. Maybe nobody's. Or everybody's. Anyway, it doesn't matter.

For about ten minutes my parents remained civil by speaking only to me. I was in the middle of two conversations, one with Dad and one with Mom. Dad asked a question about the hospital, and I answered him. Then Mom told me about a phone conversation she'd had with Mrs. Pike, and I asked her a question about Mallory. And so on.

Things began to go downhill when Dad said, "So what on earth happened this morning, Boontsie?"

To my surprise, Mom answered him before I could. "If you'd been here you'd know yourself."

"I was *work*ing," said Dad testily. "Besides, I thought we agreed not to visit Stacey together. You said you didn't want to see me."

Mom ignored that last comment. "You were working on Saturday?"

"Yes, I was working on Saturday. If I don't do my job properly, I'll get fired and then I'll lose my insurance. Do you think we could afford to have such good care for Stacey if I didn't have insurance?"

"What a hero," muttered Mom.

"Excuse me?" said Dad.

"Nothing."

"Nothing worth repeating," I spoke up.

For a moment, Mom and Dad looked at me as if they'd forgotten I was there. Or as if they'd forgotten I was their daughter. Then they picked up the argument again.

"Hospital care is not cheap," said Dad.

"I know that. So why did you put Stacey in a private room?"

"Because I love her."

"Are you saying I don't?"

"All I'm saying is that last weekend Stacey arrived in New York from Stoneybrook looking sicker than I've seen her since she was first diagnosed."

I felt my cheeks redden hotly.

"So?" Mom prompted Dad. She was trying to force him into saying something, but I'm not sure what the something was.

Dad remained silent.

"If Stacey got sick, that wasn't *my* fault," Mom finally said. "You know as well as I do that the doctors weren't sure what course this particular kind of diabetes would take. Stacey is a *brittle* diabetic. The doctors have had trouble controlling her blood sugar from the start. Plus, she's had the flu, and you know what infections can do to her. It's a miracle she hasn't — "

Mom was cut off. By me. "Shut up!"

"Anastasia," my father said warningly.

"You shut up, too!" I cried, even though I know that neither of my parents is fond of that term. And that certainly no one likes to be told to shut up.

Mom and Dad just stared at me.

I went one step further. "And get out of here. Right now. I'm not kidding."

A look of surprise, then anger, then confusion crossed Mom's face. "Stacey."

"I mean it. Get out. I thought maybe the three of us could be together for fifteen minutes without an argument, but I guess not."

Dad stood up slowly. "You were not," he said in a low voice, "brought up to speak to *any*body that way, young lady. Whether you're sick or well."

"I know," I replied after a few moments. I glanced at my mother. She was crying. And both she and Dad were gathering their things together, putting on their coats. But they looked like they were moving in slow motion.

I watched them until they were almost ready to leave. Just as they were about to walk out the door, I spoke up. "I'm sorry," I said. "I'm *so* sorry. But you guys should listen to yourselves sometime."

Mom dabbed at her eyes with a tissue. My father fumbled around for a handkerchief. I couldn't believe it. I'd made *him* cry, too. For

115

a moment, I felt the anger rise up all over again: I had the power to move two adults to tears, but not to make them act civilly toward one another.

I pushed the anger away. "Can you," I said to Mom and Dad in a steady voice, "come back on Monday, instead of tomorrow? I need some time to think."

"So do I," said Dad.

"So do I," said Mom.

"Okay. So I'll see you on Monday?"

My parents nodded. Then they left, Mom slightly ahead of Dad. I watched them to see if Dad might rest his hand on Mom's back. Or if Mom might send a flicker of a smile to Dad. But they were isolated, living in separate worlds.

Ordinarily, after a scene like that, I would have given into tears. I might even have enjoyed them, let them run down my cheeks in salty tracks, not bothered to wipe them away. Not that night, though. I was feeling too angry. And, I realized, too strong. My body was getting better, so I allowed my mind to get better, too.

"Look out for number one," I murmured. Where had I heard that? I wasn't sure. But I did, suddenly, know what it meant. And that's exactly what I was doing — looking out for number one, for *me*. I was putting me first, along with my thoughts, feelings, and emotions.

How, I wondered, did I *really* want to spend Sunday? Out of the hospital, I answered myself. But that wasn't possible. Okay. Next best thing? With my friends, forgetting about my parents. Well, *that* might be possible. I could find out in just a few minutes, with two or three phone calls.

I dialed Claudia first, praying that she was home.

She was. She answered on the first ring. "Hi, Dawn," she said.

I paused. "Claud, it's me."

"*Stacey?!* I was expecting Dawn to call me back. She — Oh, never mind. It's a long story. How are you? You sound okay. I mean, you sound *good.*"

"I'm feeling pretty good," I said truthfully. "And I was wondering something. I know this is a lot to ask, but would you and Dawn and everyone want to come back tomorrow? Would your parents let you?"

"Come *back?* To New *York?* Well . . . sure. I mean, I guess so. I mean, yes, definitely, but I have to see if we have enough money and everything."

I laughed. "I know what you mean. If you guys could come, I would *love* to see you. But I know that's asking a lot."

"Not so much," replied Claud. "Let me talk to the others. I'll get back to you."

"Okay," I replied. "I'm going to call Laine in the meantime. You don't mind, do you? I mean, if Laine comes over for awhile tomorrow? I thought it would be fun if we all got together."

"Fine with me," said Claud.

We hung up then, and I dialed Laine.

"Hi," I said. "It's Stacey. Um, is my mom back yet?"

"No," Laine answered.

"Oh. Well, she probably will be soon. And she might be uspet." I told Laine what had happened earlier.

"Wow," said Laine when I'd finished. "So do you want her to call you when she gets here?"

"No," I replied. "I really do need to wait awhile until I talk to my parents again. But I was wondering if you could visit tomorrow. Claudia and everyone might be here, too. If they get permission from their parents, and if they can get by the nurses."

"Great!" exclaimed Laine. "See you tomorrow."

On Sunday I woke up early. *Every*one had permission to visit. (Well, not Mallory and Jessi, but the others. Plus Laine. I couldn't wait.)

I asked a nurse to help me wash my hair in the sink. Then I put on fresh clothes. I even put on some makeup that Laine had sneaked to me a few days earlier. I added jewelry and, when I checked myself in the mirror, thought I looked like the same old Stacey. The same old reasonably *healthy* Stacey.

By one o'clock everyone had arrived. Laine and my Stoneybrook friends greeted each other happily. (They'd met before.) Then they all found seats (Kristy and Mary Anne refused to sit in the plastic chairs again, so they perched on the bed with Laine, while Claud and Dawn risked the chairs.)

"Guess what," I said. "I never opened my presents yesterday." I pointed to a corner where one of the nurses had hastily stacked the boxes and packages while my friends were being ushered out of the room.

"Good. Open them now," said Claud.

At that moment, a nurse entered my room.

"Aughhh!" exclaimed Mary Anne in a muffled shriek. "Another blood test?"

"No," said the nurse, smiling. "A guest check. I see you have . . ."

Her voice trailed off as she looked at me. My face was practically pleading with her. "Please, please, *please* let everyone stay," it was saying.

119

"I see that you have," the nurse began again, "exactly two visitors."

"Oh, thank you," I said, letting out the breath I'd been holding.

"You're welcome. Just don't make too much noise, okay?"

"No problem," I replied.

The nurse disappeared. "We're safe," I announced in a loud whisper.

"Good. Open the presents," said Claud. She piled them on my bed. They tumbled around Laine and Kristy and Mary Anne.

I reached for one. But Claud moved it away. "How about this one?" she asked, handing me another.

"Okay," I said. I looked at the tag. "Why, it's from *you!*"

Everybody giggled.

Claudia's present was a beaded bracelet that she'd made herself.

"Thanks!" I exclaimed as I slipped it on.

That was the beginning of an afternoon of (quiet) fun.

I even managed to forget about Mom and Dad.

CHAPTER 14

Thursday

I sat for Charlotte this evening, and she came down with (in this order) Lyme disease, arthritis, a kidney problem, and a strep throat. It's hard to be annoyed with her, though. I think she really doesn't feel one hundred percent these days. I also think that's because she's tired. Every night she lies awake worrying about Stacey.

Well, by the end of this evening, her worries were over -- and she had made a miraculous recovery, considering that the last *time I had a strep throat I missed a week and a half of school.*

What cured Charlotte? A phone call from Claudia, that's what. And I should add that anyone who heard from Claud tonight felt better when they got off the phone . . . .

"Mary Anne?" said Charlotte plaintively.

"Yeah?" replied Mary Anne.

"I don't feel good."

It was about eight o'clock on Thursday evening. Mary Anne had been at the Johanssens' for half an hour. When she had arrived, Charlotte was already in her nightgown, sitting on her bed, looking slightly pale.

Mary Anne did not panic when Charlotte said she wasn't feeling well. She knew what was going on with Char. So she said calmly, "How don't you feel good?"

"I'm sort of achey. And I'm *really* tired. I think my neck is getting stiff. I probably have Lyme disease. We'll know for sure if a rash appears where I've been bitten by the tick. Of course, a rash doesn't always show up. Then you have to get a blood test or something."

"Char, when was the last time you played in the woods?"

Charlotte paused. "I don't remember," she said after a moment. "But that doesn't matter, you know. Carrot spends lots of time outdoors." (Carrot is the Johanssens' schnauzer.) "He could bring deer ticks into the house. I could have been bitten right here in my bedroom."

Mary Anne didn't know what to say to that.

I could sympathize. When my parents had come back to the hospital (separately) on Monday, I hadn't been sure what to say to *them*. The night before, I had thought of some things I wanted to say, like, "Don't put me in the middle," or, "Let the *doctors* talk about my disease. They're the experts, not you."

But did I say those things? No. I was too chicken. All I could do was apologize over and over again. "I'm sorry," I kept saying. "I don't know how I could have told you to shut up and to get out."

"Well, you were upset," said Dad.

"You weren't feeling well," said Mom.

"That's true. . . ." But those weren't the most important reasons behind what I'd said. The important reasons were much more complicated. By Thursday, when Mary Anne was sitting for Charlotte, my parents and I had gotten over Saturday. We were no longer angry. Mom and Dad had accepted my apologies. But I wasn't much closer to telling them what was *really* wrong than I had been before our fight. However, I was thinking all the time. I knew that when I was ready, I would have plenty to say and that I would say it without getting angry or upset.

At any rate, it didn't matter that Mary Anne had no calming words for Charlotte. That's because Char was *convinced* she had Lyme disease. There was no talking her out of it. Besides, while Mary Anne was still coming up with something to say, Charlotte shrieked suddenly and pointed to the rug.

"What's wrong?" asked Mary Anne, alarmed.

"I see a deer tick! Right here in my room. Now do you believe me?"

"Where's the tick?" Mary Anne was slightly annoyed.

"Right there," Char answered, still pointing to the rug.

Mary Anne peered at the floor. "That little thing?" Her eyes had finally rested on a tiny black dot working its way from one side of the room to the other.

"Deer ticks are small," Charlotte informed

Mary Anne. "No bigger than the period at the end of a sentence."

Mary Anne is not crazy about bugs, but she examined the moving speck from short range. At last she said, "Char, that is not a tick. It's a very small spider."

"How can you tell?"

"It's too big to be a deer tick. Besides, it just *looks* like a spider."

"Oh. Well, can you get rid of it?"

"I won't kill it, if that's what you mean," Mary Anne replied. "But I'll put it outside. I'll set it free."

"Okay," agreed Charlotte. And by the time Mary Anne had set the spider outdoors, Charlotte had another complaint. "You know, I really think I might have arthritis," she said when Mary Anne returned. "My back hurts. People can get arthritis in their backs, you know. . . . Or, wait! I bet I have a kidney disease. People sometimes get backaches when they have a kidney infection."

"They also run fevers." Mary Anne touched Char's forehead. "And you don't have one."

Charlotte was silent for awhile. Finally she said, "Let's read, Mary Anne. Let's read about . . . " Charlotte scanned her bookshelf. Then she asked Mary Anne if there were any new books in her Kid-Kit.

"Just one," answered Mary Anne. She

fished around in the box until she found a copy of *The Five Little Peppers and How They Grew*, which is a story about the Pepper family, not a bunch of vegetables.

"Ooh, that looks good," said Char.

"It is. I think you'll like it. Do you want me to start reading?"

Charlotte nodded. She snuggled against Mary Anne. But Mary Anne hadn't read more than four pages when Charlotte interrupted her.

"Mary Anne? My throat is really sore."

"Maybe you should gargle," suggested Mary Anne.

"Maybe," said Charlotte. "But I don't know if gargling will help a strep throat."

Mary Anne closed her eyes briefly. Just as she was opening them, ready for yet another talk with Charlotte, the phone rang. Mary Anne ran downstairs to answer it. (She *could* have answered the upstairs phone, but Mary Anne feels funny about entering Dr. and Mr. Johanssen's bedrooom. Or any other grown-up's bedroom, for that matter.)

"Hello, Johanssens' residence," said Mary Anne.

"Hi, it's Claud," said Claudia, "and I have some news about Stacey."

"News? What's happened?" Mary Anne asked quickly. Was this good news or bad

news? Had I had another relapse? she wondered. Were my new shots working the way
they should be?

"Okay, get this," said Claud. "Stacey will
be home on Saturday."

"All *right!*" cried Mary Anne. "Just two
more days. Wait till I tell Charlotte. She will
be so happy! You can't imagine."

"Oh, yes, I can!" exclaimed Claudia. "And
tell Char that when Stacey returns she'll have
to rest for a week, then she can go back to
school, and a week after *that* she can start
baby-sitting again."

"Terrific!" said Mary Anne.

"I'm calling all the BSC members," added
Claud, "so I better go now."

Mary Anne hung up the phone then and
raced to Charlotte's room. "Guess what! Guess
what!" she cried. "No, you won't guess, so
I'll tell you."

"Yeah?" said Charlotte.

"Stacey will be home in two days."

"Aughhh!" shrieked Charlotte. (Mary Anne
decided that Char's throat wasn't bothering
her *too* much.) "On Saturday? Stacey will be
back on Saturday?"

"Yup," said Mary Anne. She told Charlotte
what Claud had said about resting, school,
and baby-sitting.

"So Stacey can't baby-sit me for over two weeks?"

"That's right. But isn't it nice to know she's coming back here?"

"Definitely," said Char. "You know what? We should do something for Stacey. We should give her a surprise party."

"I don't know about a surprise party, since Stacey is supposed to be resting, but we should do *some*thing for her. She'd like that."

"Then let's give her a regular party. We won't surprise her."

"A small, quiet regular party, maybe," said Mary Anne.

"We could make a sign," suggested Charlotte. "I mean, a banner. Remember the banner we hung up when Stacey and her mom moved back to Stoneybrook?"

"Yup. We hung it in front of her house. We could do that again."

"And then we'll be waiting for her in the front yard when her mother drives her home. Only we won't jump out or anything. And we won't invite as many people as we did the last time."

"That sounds good. And maybe we'll just drag over the Pikes' picnic table and serve juice or lemonade."

"Lemonade without sugar in it," added Charlotte.

"Right," said Mary Anne. "Or with artificial sweeteners. Okay, this sounds good. The party will be quiet and small. I think Stacey will really like it. What should the banner say?"

Charlotte frowned. "Mmm . . . how about, 'We're glad you're home, Stacey'?"

"Perfect!"

"Really?" Charlotte looked very pleased.

"Positively. Do you want to help make the banner?"

"Positively!" replied Charlotte, grinning.

"I should call Claudia and everyone and see what they think about this."

"Call them right now," said Charlotte.

"Okay." Mary Anne headed back downstairs.

Charlotte ran after her. "Hey, guess what! My strep throat is gone! And I'm pretty sure I don't have Lyme disease or arthritis, or anything, either."

Mary Anne turned around. She hugged Charlotte. "You don't know how glad I am to hear that," she said.

"Who should we call first?" asked Charlotte, wriggling out of Mary Anne's grasp.

"Claudia, I think," answered Mary Anne. "She's got paint. We'll probably make the banner at her house tomorrow afternoon."

"I'll dial!" exclaimed Char.

So she did. Then she handed the receiver to Mary Anne. Mary Anne spoke to Claud, who loved the idea of welcoming me home. Within fifteen minutes, Dawn, Mal, Jessi, and Kristy knew about the party, too. Mary Anne assigned jobs to everyone. My friends could not wait for Saturday — and neither could I!

CHAPTER 15

The highway stretched in front of us. I imagined it was the Yellow Brick Road, and that it led straight to my house.

Saturday had arrived at last. I had been sprung from the hospital. And now that I was out of that bland room with its view of dingy gray, I really did feel like Dorothy in Oz. "Hey, Mom, there are *colors* out here!" I had exclaimed as a nurse helped me into our car.

Mom laughed.

The nurse smiled. "It was nice knowing you, Stacey," she said, "but I don't ever want to see your face here again!" (She didn't?) "Don't worry," the nurse went on, "I say that to all my patients. Stay well, okay?"

It was my turn to smile. "Okay." I paused. Then I added, "I hope *I* never see *your* face again, either!"

Grinning, the nurse turned the empty wheelchair around and started toward the door of the hospital.

"Why do they always make me leave the hospital in a wheelchair?" I complained. "I can walk. I was walking in the hospital."

Mom shrugged. "Just hospital policy, sweetie." She turned the key in the ignition and at last I began to leave the hospital behind me.

The morning had been a little hectic. Mom arrived early to pack my suitcase, and to put all of my cards and gifts into shopping bags. Then she began to empty a vase of its flowers.

"Mom!" I exclaimed. "Can't we keep my flowers? Can't we take them home?"

"*All* of them?" replied Mom. The room was overflowing.

"Well, some of them," I said. "Maybe we could give the rest to the nurses or to the other kids here."

"Good idea," Mom had answered.

So we'd left two bouquets of flowers at the nurses' station. We had delivered four more bouquets to the kids I'd gotten to know the best (which wasn't very well), and we took three home with us.

While Mom was running around packing my suitcase and handing out flowers, Dad arrived to say good-bye to me. He knew that Mom would be there, and Mom knew that

132

Dad was coming, so when they found themselves together in my room, they didn't talk, but they didn't argue, either.

"From now on," said Dad, "be sure to tell your mother or me when you're feeling so awful. You know the signs to look for."

"Yeah," I agreed. "I guess I wasn't very responsible."

Dad shook his head. "It wasn't your fault," he said.

"Then whose was it?"

Dad shrugged. "What difference does it make?"

"None, I guess."

A little while later, Dad and I were hugging good-bye.

"I promise that my next visit will be more fun," I said.

"I should hope so," Dad answered, smiling. "This'll be hard to top in terms of rotten vacations."

"There's always the sewage treatment plant," I said. "Maybe we could tour it the next time I come for a weekend."

"Okay," said my father. "Then we'll finish off the day with a ride on a garbage barge. We'll try to pick a hot, sunny afternoon so the garbage will be particularly disgusting and smelly."

"Dad, you are so gross!" I cried.

"That's what fathers are for," he replied, as he left my room.

When he was gone, Mom and I waited around for a doctor to come give me a final examination. Then we could . . . leave!

Now it was sometime in the early afternoon, and Mom and I were following the Yellow Brick Road back to our house on Elm Street in Stoneybrook, Connecticut. My eyes drooped as we drove along.

The next thing I knew, Mom was gently shaking my shoulder.

"We're almost home, Stace," she said.

"Okay," I replied groggily. Why was Mom waking me up? I would wake up by myself when she parked the car in — "I don't believe it!" I cried.

Mom turned to smile at me, "Everyone's glad you've come back."

"I guess so!"

We were turning the corner onto our street, and already I could see a bunch of balloons tied to our mailbox. And standing in the yard was a small crowd of kids. As we pulled closer, I could see all my BSC friends, Charlotte, Becca Ramsey, Jamie Newton, Myriah and Gabbie Perkins, and several of Mallory's brothers and sisters.

And then I saw the banner: WE'RE GLAD

YOU'RE HOME, STACEY! It had been hung across the front door. "I don't believe it," I said again.

Mom pulled into the driveway. "Your public awaits you," she said.

Slowly I got out of our car. As soon as I stood up, everybody began yelling and cheering and calling to me.

"Hi!" I cried.

And then there was this rush of bodies. I ran around the front of the car ("Slow down, Stacey," said Mom) and all the kids ran toward me. Soon I was hugging everyone, except the Pike triplets, who said they would die if a girl touched them.

"I'm so glad you're home," said Claudia.

"Oh, me, too!" I replied.

I looked down to see who was hugging my waist. It was Charlotte.

"I didn't really think you'd come back," she said. "But you're all well now."

The truth was, I would never be *all* well, but I didn't think this was the appropriate time to say so to Charlotte.

Mary Anne was standing at a picnic table. She ladled lemonade into paper cups, and the kids passed them around. I sat down on the front stoop to drink mine — after I checked to make sure that it didn't contain any *real* sugar.

"Tired, Stace?" asked Dawn.

"Yeah," I admitted.

So Dawn broke up the party then. She sent the guests home, except for Claudia. By this time, Mom had emptied the car. She had carried the suitcase and shopping bags and vases of flowers inside.

"I think I'm going to lie down for awhile," I told Claud.

"Are you going to nap?" she asked.

"No. Just rest. Come with me, okay?"

Claud nodded. "Sure."

We stepped into my house. I breathed in deeply. "Ahhh. This certainly smells better than the hospital did."

Claudia giggled. "Come along, patient," she said.

"Okay, Nurse Claudia." I turned around. "Mom, Claudia and I are going upstairs!" I called.

"All right," my mother called back.

"I think I'm actually going to get *in* bed," I told Claud as we trudged upstairs. When we reached my room, I opened my window. "Fresh air," I murmured. Then I glanced around. "You don't know how nice it is to see colors other than gray and white."

I opened a drawer and took out a clean nightgown.

"Oh, yes, I do," Claud replied, thinking of her own stay in the hospital after she'd broken her leg.

I changed into my nightgown and crawled into bed. Claudia and I gabbed until I started to fall asleep.

"I'll call you later," said Claud as she left.

"Okay. Thanks." I drifted off to sleep, thinking, There's no place like home. There's no place like home.

I slept for several hours. When I woke up, I felt well enough to eat dinner in the kitchen with Mom. But after that, I was tired again.

"I think I'll go to bed soon," I told my mother. "But first, can you come upstairs so we can talk?"

"Of course." Mom followed me back to my room, where I crawled under the covers again. She sat on the edge of my bed.

"This is something I've been trying to tell you and Dad for a long time now," I began. I drew in a deep breath. "Okay. Here's the thing. I am not going to be the monkey for you guys anymore."

"The monkey?"

"Yeah. I feel like the monkey in monkey-in-the-middle. Dad's always trying to get information about you from me. And you try to find out about Dad from me. And both of you send nasty messages through me. That's not fair. So from now on, I'm not talking about you to Dad or about Dad to you, and I'm not delivering any messages. I'll call Dad in a few minutes and tell him all this, too."

"Okay," said Mom, nodding her head. "So far what you've said seems reasonable."

"I also want to apologize," I went on. "I know I've been crabby lately, but I wasn't feeling well. Plus, I guess I've been mad at you guys."

"Apology accepted. And *my* apologies to you for making you feel like a monkey."

I smiled. "Thanks. When I call Dad, I'll also tell him that I'll visit him more often, and without any arguments. I'll be happy to go to New York when I'm feeling better and when I know I won't be the monkey."

"Fair enough," said Mom.

"One last thing. I have to make a confession." I paused because I could feel tears coming to my eyes. "Um, I'm really sorry about all this, but I think the reason I went into the hospital was that I stopped following my diet." I told my mother about the fudge and the candy and everything.

Then I began to cry.

Mom put her arms around me. "Honey," she said softly, "you shouldn't have done that, but the doctors are pretty sure your diet didn't have much to do with the change in your blood sugar level. You haven't been feeling well for a long time now, have you?"

I shook my head. "No, I haven't." I was still crying.

"And you know that being a diabetic, especially with this kind of juvenile-onset diabetes, you're much more susceptible to infections than other people are. Plus, because diabetes can be a mean disease, once you've gotten an infection, then you're more open to problems with your insulin. It's a vicious cycle. We've been lucky so far, but lately you've had the flu and a sore throat — "

"And bronchitis, remember?"

"That's right. I'd forgotten. Furthermore, you've been incredibly busy. So I'm sure that eating the sweets didn't help anything, but I'm also sure that that's not why you got sick."

I had stopped crying. I pulled away from Mom. "Maybe I should slow down a little," I told her.

"Good idea."

"I need to catch up on my schoolwork anyway. And the next time I'm not feeling well, I'll tell you. That way I can see the doctor before I get so sick."

"Another good idea."

"Thank you," I said again. I kissed Mom. "I'm really tired," I told her, "but I have to do one more thing before I go to bed."

I stood up. Then I went into Mom's room. It was time to talk to my father.

Dear Reader,

Lots of people have asked me why I created a character with diabetes. The answer to that question is that two of my friends are diabetic, so I knew a bit about the illness because of them. Of course, once the series began, I learned as much as I could about diabetes so that I could write about it realistically.

A number of books in the Baby-sitters Club series have dealt with medical issues. Anytime I write a book like that, I ask a doctor friend of mine to review it. Guess what? My friend is Claudia Werner, for whom Claudia Kishi was named.

Ironically, eight years after the series began, my cat Mouse developed diabetes, so I had firsthand experience with the illness. Mouse needed two insulin injections each day, and I had to monitor his food, water, and insulin intake very carefully. This was nothing like what Stacey has to go through, but it did give me more insight into the challenges she faces. Incidentally, for years Stacey has been one of the most popular characters in the series. I think it is because readers admire her courage and determination.

Happy reading,

Ann M Martin

Ann M. Martin

About the Author

ANN MATTHEWS MARTIN was born on August 12, 1955. She grew up in Princeton, NJ, with her parents and her younger sister, Jane.

Although Ann used to be a teacher and then an editor of children's books, she's now a full-time writer. She gets the ideas for her books from many different places. Some are based on personal experiences. Others are based on childhood memories and feelings. Many are written about contemporary problems or events.

All of Ann's characters, even the members of the Baby-sitters Club, are made up. (So is Stoneybrook.) But many of her characters are based on real people. Sometimes Ann names her characters after people she knows, other times she chooses names she likes.

In addition to the Baby-sitters Club books, Ann Martin has written many other books for children. Her favorite is *Ten Kids, No Pets* because she loves big families and she loves animals. Her favorite Baby-sitters Club book is *Kristy's Big Day*. (By the way, Kristy is her favorite baby-sitter!)

Ann M. Martin now lives in New York with her cats, Gussie and Woody. Her hobbies are reading, sewing, and needlework — especially making clothes for children.

Notebook Pages

This Baby-sitters Club book belongs to _Jessie_.

I am _8_ years old and in the _3_ grade.

The name of my school is _F·W·S_.

I got this BSC book from _____.

I started reading it on _____ and

finished reading it on _____.

The place where I read most of this book is _____.

My favorite part was when _____.

If I could change anything in the story, it might be the part when

_____.

My favorite character in the Baby-sitters Club is _Kristy is_.

The BSC member I am most like is _Kristy_.

because _____.

If I could write a Baby-sitters Club book it would be about ___

_____.

#43 Stacey's Emergency

Stacey has a serious emergency when she ends up in the hospital because of her diabetes. The most serious emergency I've ever had was when _____ _____ . This is what happened: _____ _____ _____ . Because she has diabetes, Stacey has to be very careful about what and when she eats. Some things I have to be very careful about are _____ _____ _____ .

In *Stacey's Emergency*, Stacey has many things to worry about — from her parents' fights to her difficult schoolwork. Some of the things I worry about are _____ _____ _____ _____ . But I feel better when I think about _____ _____ _____ .

STACEY'S

Here I am, age three.

Me with Charlotte
my "almost

A family portrait — me
with my parents.

SCRAPBOOK

Johanssen,
sister."

Getting ready for school.

In LUV at Shadow Lake.

Read all the books
about **Stacey**
in the Baby-sitters Club series
by Ann M. Martin

3 *The Truth About Stacey*
Stacey's different . . . and it's harder on her than
anyone knows.

8 *Boy-Crazy Stacey*
Who needs baby-sitting when there are boys
around!

#13 *Good-bye Stacey, Good-bye*
How do you say good-bye to your very best friend?

#18 *Stacey's Mistake*
Stacey has never been so wrong in her life!

#28 *Welcome Back, Stacey!*
Stacey's moving again . . . back to Stoneybrook!

#35 *Stacey and the Mystery of Stoneybrook*
Stacey discovers a *haunted house* in Stoneybrook!

#43 *Stacey's Emergency*
The Baby-sitters are so worried. Something's
wrong with Stacey.

#51 *Stacey's Ex-Best Friend*
Is Stacey's old friend Laine super mature or just a
super snob?

#58 *Stacey's Choice*
Stacey's parents are both depending on her. But
how can she choose between them . . . again?

#65 *Stacey's Big Crush*
Stacey's in LUV . . . with her twenty-two-year-old
teacher!

#70 *Stacey and the Cheerleaders*
Stacey becomes part of the "in" crowd when she
tries out for the cheerleading team.

#76 Stacey's Lie
    When Stacey tells one lie it turns to another, then
    another, then another . . .

#83 Stacey vs. the BSC
    Is Stacey outgrowing the BSC?

#87 Stacey and the Bad Girls
    With friends like these, who needs enemies?

#94 Stacey McGill, Super Sitter
    It's a bird . . . it's a plane . . . it's a super sitter!

#99 Stacey's Broken Heart
    Who will pick up the pieces?

Mysteries:

 # 1 Stacey and the Missing Ring
    Stacey has to find that ring — or business is over
    for the Baby-sitters Club!

#10 Stacey and the Mystery Money
    Who would give Stacey counterfeit money?

#14 Stacey and the Mystery at the Mall
    Shoplifting, burglaries — mysterious things are
    going on at the Washington Mall!

#18 Stacey and the Mystery at the Empty House
    Stacey enjoys house-sitting for the Johanssens —
    until she thinks someone's hiding out in the house.

#22 Stacey and the Haunted Masquerade
    This is one dance that Stacey will *never* forget!

Portrait Collection:

Stacey's Book
    An autobiography of the BSC's big city girl.

The Baby-sitters Club®

Collect 'em all!

100 (and more) Reasons to Stay Friends Forever!

❑ MG43388-1	#1	Kristy's Great Idea	$3.50
❑ MG43387-3	#10	Logan Likes Mary Anne!	$3.99
❑ MG43717-8	#15	Little Miss Stoneybrook...and Dawn	$3.50
❑ MG43722-4	#20	Kristy and the Walking Disaster	$3.50
❑ MG43347-4	#25	Mary Anne and the Search for Tigger	$3.50
❑ MG42498-X	#30	Mary Anne and the Great Romance	$3.50
❑ MG42508-0	#35	Stacey and the Mystery of Stoneybrook	$3.50
❑ MG44082-9	#40	Claudia and the Middle School Mystery	$3.25
❑ MG43574-4	#45	Kristy and the Baby Parade	$3.50
❑ MG44969-9	#50	Dawn's Big Date	$3.50
❑ MG44968-0	#51	Stacey's Ex-Best Friend	$3.50
❑ MG44966-4	#52	Mary Anne + 2 Many Babies	$3.50
❑ MG44967-2	#53	Kristy for President	$3.25
❑ MG44965-6	#54	Mallory and the Dream Horse	$3.25
❑ MG44964-8	#55	Jessi's Gold Medal	$3.25
❑ MG45657-1	#56	Keep Out, Claudia!	$3.50
❑ MG45658-X	#57	Dawn Saves the Planet	$3.50
❑ MG45659-8	#58	Stacey's Choice	$3.50
❑ MG45660-1	#59	Mallory Hates Boys (and Gym)	$3.50
❑ MG45662-8	#60	Mary Anne's Makeover	$3.50
❑ MG45663-6	#61	Jessi and the Awful Secret	$3.50
❑ MG45664-4	#62	Kristy and the Worst Kid Ever	$3.50
❑ MG45665-2	#63	Claudia's Special Friend	$3.50
❑ MG45666-0	#64	Dawn's Family Feud	$3.50
❑ MG45667-9	#65	Stacey's Big Crush	$3.50
❑ MG47004-3	#66	Maid Mary Anne	$3.50
❑ MG47005-1	#67	Dawn's Big Move	$3.50
❑ MG47006-X	#68	Jessi and the Bad Baby-sitter	$3.50
❑ MG47007-8	#69	Get Well Soon, Mallory!	$3.50
❑ MG47008-6	#70	Stacey and the Cheerleaders	$3.50
❑ MG47009-4	#71	Claudia and the Perfect Boy	$3.99
❑ MG47010-8	#72	Dawn and the We Love Kids Club	$3.99
❑ MG47011-6	#73	Mary Anne and Miss Priss	$3.99
❑ MG47012-4	#74	Kristy and the Copycat	$3.99
❑ MG47013-2	#75	Jessi's Horrible Prank	$3.50
❑ MG47014-0	#76	Stacey's Lie	$3.50
❑ MG48221-1	#77	Dawn and Whitney, Friends Forever	$3.99
❑ MG48222-X	#78	Claudia and Crazy Peaches	$3.50
❑ MG48223-8	#79	Mary Anne Breaks the Rules	$3.50
❑ MG48224-6	#80	Mallory Pike, #1 Fan	$3.99

More titles... ▶

The Baby-sitters Club titles continued...

❏ MG48225-4	#81	Kristy and Mr. Mom	$3.50
❏ MG48226-2	#82	Jessi and the Troublemaker	$3.99
❏ MG48235-1	#83	Stacey vs. the BSC	$3.50
❏ MG48228-9	#84	Dawn and the School Spirit War	$3.50
❏ MG48236-X	#85	Claudi Kishi, Live from WSTO	$3.50
❏ MG48227-0	#86	Mary Anne and Camp BSC	$3.50
❏ MG48237-8	#87	Stacey and the Bad Girls	$3.50
❏ MG22872-2	#88	Farewell, Dawn	$3.50
❏ MG22873-0	#89	Kristy and the Dirty Diapers	$3.50
❏ MG22874-9	#90	Welcome to the BSC, Abby	$3.50
❏ MG22875-1	#91	Claudia and the First Thanksgiving	$3.50
❏ MG22876-5	#92	Mallory's Christmas Wish	$3.50
❏ MG22877-3	#93	Mary Anne and the Memory Garden	$3.99
❏ MG22878-1	#94	Stacey McGill, Super Sitter	$3.99
❏ MG22879-X	#95	Kristy + Bart = ?	$3.99
❏ MG22880-3	#96	Abby's Lucky Thirteen	$3.99
❏ MG22881-1	#97	Claudia and the World's Cutest Baby	$3.99
❏ MG22882-X	#98	Dawn and Too Many Baby-sitters	$3.99
❏ MG69205-4	#99	Stacey's Broken Heart	$3.99
❏ MG69206-2	#100	Kristy's Worst Idea	$3.99
❏ MG45575-3		Logan's Story Special Edition Readers' Request	$3.25
❏ MG47118-X		Logan Bruno, Boy Baby-sitter	
		Special Edition Readers' Request	$3.50
❏ MG47756-0		Shannon's Story Special Edition	$3.50
❏ MG47686-6		The Baby-sitters Club Guide to Baby-sitting	$3.25
❏ MG47314-X		The Baby-sitters Club Trivia and Puzzle Fun Book	$2.50
❏ MG48400-1		BSC Portrait Collection: Claudia's Book	$3.50
❏ MG22864-1		BSC Portrait Collection: Dawn's Book	$3.50
❏ MG69181-3		BSC Portrait Collection: Kristy's Book	$3.99
❏ MG22865-X		BSC Portrait Collection: Mary Anne's Book	$3.99
❏ MG48399-4		BSC Portrait Collection: Stacey's Book	$3.50
❏ MG92713-2		The Complete Guide to the Baby-sitters Club	$4.95
❏ MG47151-1		The Baby-sitters Club Chain Letter	$14.95
❏ MG48295-5		The Baby-sitters Club Secret Santa	$14.95
❏ MG45074-3		The Baby-sitters Club Notebook	$2.50
❏ MG44783-1		The Baby-sitters Club Postcard Book	$4.95

Available wherever you buy books...or use this order form.
Scholastic Inc., P.O. Box 7502, 2931 E. McCarty Street, Jefferson City, MO 65102

Please send me the books I have checked above. I am enclosing $_____
(please add $2.00 to cover shipping and handling). Send check or money order–
no cash or C.O.D.s please.

Name_____ Birthdate_____

Address _____

City_____ State/Zip _____

Please allow four to six weeks for delivery. Offer good in the U.S. only. Sorry,
mail orders are not available to residents of Canada. Prices subject to change.

BSC596

THE BABY-SITTERS CLUB®

by Ann M. Martin

Collect and read these exciting BSC Super Specials, Mysteries, and Super Mysteries along with your favorite Baby-sitters Club books!

BSC Super Specials

❏ BBK44240-6	Baby-sitters on Board! Super Special #1	$3.95
❏ BBK44239-2	Baby-sitters' Summer Vacation Super Special #2	$3.95
❏ BBK43973-1	Baby-sitters' Winter Vacation Super Special #3	$3.95
❏ BBK42493-9	Baby-sitters' Island Adventure Super Special #4	$3.95
❏ BBK43575-2	California Girls! Super Special #5	$3.95
❏ BBK43576-0	New York, New York! Super Special #6	$4.50
❏ BBK44963-X	Snowbound! Super Special #7	$3.95
❏ BBK44962-X	Baby-sitters at Shadow Lake Super Special #8	$3.95
❏ BBK45661-X	Starring The Baby-sitters Club! Super Special #9	$3.95
❏ BBK45674-1	Sea City, Here We Come! Super Special #10	$3.95
❏ BBK47015-9	The Baby-sitters Remember Super Special #11	$3.95
❏ BBK48308-0	Here Come the Bridesmaids! Super Special #12	$3.95
❏ BBK22883-8	Aloha, Baby-sitters! Super Special #13	$4.50

BSC Mysteries

❏ BAI44084-5	#1 Stacey and the Missing Ring	$3.50
❏ BAI44085-3	#2 Beware Dawn!	$3.50
❏ BAI44799-8	#3 Mallory and the Ghost Cat	$3.50
❏ BAI44800-5	#4 Kristy and the Missing Child	$3.50
❏ BAI44801-3	#5 Mary Anne and the Secret in the Attic	$3.50
❏ BAI44961-3	#6 The Mystery at Claudia's House	$3.50
❏ BAI44960-5	#7 Dawn and the Disappearing Dogs	$3.50
❏ BAI44959-1	#8 Jessi and the Jewel Thieves	$3.50
❏ BAI44958-3	#9 Kristy and the Haunted Mansion	$3.50
❏ BAI45696-2	#10 Stacey and the Mystery Money	$3.50

More titles ➡